THE HOUSE ON COOPER LANE

Oliver Phipps

Gray Door

Gray Door Ltd.

ISBN 978-0-9896012-3-8

Table of Contents

Introduction

The incidents relayed in this book are all based on actual events in my life. Names have been changed, and the timing of the occurrences has been adjusted into a more suitable framework for the story. The events themselves happened, and I endeavored only to make changes necessary for keeping congruency.

Thank you, and I hope you enjoy *The House on Cooper Lane*.

Oliver Phipps

Chapter One:

THE HOUSE

Bud pulled off the road in front of a large sign that read, "Welcome to Madison LA."

He wanted to browse through his selection of cassette tapes, as the one in the player had become wearisome many miles back. A fresh set of songs was called for, now that they'd finally reached their destination. The stop also seemed an ideal place to park and let Badger out for a bathroom break.

The 1973 Pontiac Grand Am rumbled as it idled beside the road.

"All right, boy, you ready for a little break?"

The large Doberman pinscher sat perched in the passenger seat and turned to look at his master in an almost humanlike motion. His canine friend appeared to be saying without words, "What do you think? Of course, I am."

While Badger took care of his business beside the road, Bud changed the tape. He then stretched his legs and let Badger back in; "Well, did everything go okay?"

His friend let out something of a whiny bark in frustration at his master's personal query.

"All right, let's find out what this here town has to offer in the housing department."

With the volume turned up and the windows down, the two rolled into Madison with rock and roll blaring and the warm summer air of 1984 blowing in their hair.

At nineteen years old, Bud Fisher had already been independent for several years. The recent job opportunity he'd received signaled a new prospect for the young man. He would need to travel with this company, but he didn't consider that a problem. He liked this aspect of the job. The higher pay would balance the traveling expenses as well as greatly increase his abilities in the department of self-sufficiency. His first task, however, would be to find a place to stay with his limited funds; keeping in mind he would need to work several weeks before getting his first paycheck, Bud knew he must be thrifty with his money for a while.

"Okay, at least we know where the paper mill is." As they drove down the road, Bud glanced over at a facility with smoke rising from its two large stacks. "That's where I'll need to be first thing Monday morning, so we've got to find a place to rent this weekend."

Badger looked over at his master as if he liked hearing the words, regardless of what Bud was saying. The two then stopped at a convenience store and picked up a newspaper to check for rentals.

The construction company he'd recently hired on with would be working at the paper mill for the next three to four months, so they only needed to find temporary living arrangements. The rest of the day consisted of stopping by houses with rooms to rent within Bud's price range. Of the few that hadn't already been rented, there were none that the owners were willing to rent out on a temporary basis. With the daylight growing dimmer, his hopes for finding a place to stay began to fade.

As the fruitless day transitioned into evening, Bud drove out of town and found a dirt road. He parked on the side of the desolate stretch of gravel and crawled into the back seat to try to catch some sleep. Badger squirmed around the front bucket seat in a restless effort to get comfortable.

Just as slumber began to ease the young man's mind and body, Badger passed loud and smelly gas.

"Oh man, ewwww... Badger, what did you do?"

He quickly jumped out of the car, trying to get a breath of fresher air.

"What have you been eating? Never mind. I know."

He waited until the air inside the vehicle cleared and crawled back in to try again for some sleep. With the windows down, the mosquitoes were a constant nuisance. With the windows up, the heat became unbearable. As dawn slipped over the horizon, the two were exhausted from struggling all night for a little rest.

"Well, what do you say we go try again, buddy?"

Bud stretched his sore body. He felt as if he'd flopped around in a clothes dryer all night. Badger bailed out of the car behind his master. Shaking to rid his body of the turbulent night, the dog trotted up the dirt road a ways and began

4

sniffing the side in search of a good bathroom spot. Bud decided his dog had a good idea and walked to the back of the car to answer a nature call as well.

Once again, the two rolled into town. Saturday morning, Bud thought. This time there was no music playing. He watched sternly as they moved up and down the streets, hoping for any sign of a room or small house to rent. Having exhausted all the possible rentals from the paper, he began to grow more concerned as the day wore on.

As his hopes dwindled, Bud considered renting a room at a motel, but this would take a significant portion of the money he had saved for rent.

"I don't know, boy, this seems to be the making of another night on the old dirt road."

Bud glanced at Badger, who had his tongue hanging out and was watching the scenery go by. The dog still managed to respond with a carefree whine.

The houses became larger as they moved through an older, upscale part of town.

"This must be the old 'well-to-do' neighborhood." Bud rested his left arm on the door as they slowly moved down the street. The houses stood two stories high in an old but impressive picturesque display. A sense of stepping into a grand past came over Bud as the historic old mansions rolled into view.

"I don't think there's anything for us around here." He again looked over at Badger and then at a grand old house creeping by on the right side of the road. They moved beside the house, and as they almost passed it, Bud caught a glimpse of something. He immediately stepped on the brakes causing the tires to squeal in protest.

"Wait a minute. Wait," Bud shifted the Pontiac in reverse and backed up to get a closer view.

A rectangular sign stood erect in the front yard, and Bud read "Cooper Lane Apar—" The rest of the sign remained obscured by a bush with long stringing branches. He pulled into the drive to investigate further. As he opened the door and stepped out, Badger jumped into the driver's seat and then out the door behind his master.

He ran into the overgrown lawn, which appeared not to have been mown for some time. Moving up to the sign, Bud pulled the bush back to reveal the word "Apartments."

"Hey Badger, don't do that. We don't live here yet." He cringed a little, realizing Badger had already delivered a large amount of "doggie do" on the lawn. The dog happily scampered back up to Bud as if he'd done something great.

"Oh boy, you may have just messed up our chances of getting a room here, you knucklehead." His canine friend paid no attention to this and ran around him several times in a display of apparent relief.

Walking up the steps to the large porch, Bud noticed several plant pots with dry dirt in them. Leaves and other small debris lay scattered across the weathered walkway and appeared as if no one had set foot on it for quite some time.

A large ornate door stood on the left side, and on the right end, a smaller one that resembled a newer style and of having been added onto the house at some later date. He moved to the large door and tapped the bronze knocker several times. Badger trotted up the steps and stood behind him, staring at the entryway expectantly.

After a reasonable amount of time had passed without an answer, Bud used his hand to knock again. When this produced no response, he moved down to the smaller door at the other end of the porch; his knuckles were just about to knock on the wood when he noticed a padlock about midway down. His hand retracted, and he gazed back at the larger door in a vain hope that someone may have answered. Then, he moved back down the steps of the large porch. They began walking around the right side of the vintage house.

The young man now examined the massive structure as they moved toward the back. He couldn't help but admire the lavish features that adorned the windows and trim.

The grass they moved through stood almost knee-high. As he came around the house, he found a stairway built onto the backside that allowed access to the second floor. A long walkway built along the length of the second story and doorways on both ends of the house could also be seen.

Farther behind the house, a storage building stood at the corner of the yard. A tall hedge ran along the edges of the property, concealing the houses and yards adjacent to that side of the old house.

He realized as he made his way up the stairs that this had been quite the mansion at one time but had obviously been renovated and turned into apartments at some point during its later years. The house reminded him of structures he'd seen that were built around the turn of the century. The newer alterations weren't very becoming, but the mansion still held onto an air of dignity nonetheless.

Badger reluctantly followed his master up the stairs with his toenails scratching and searching for a grip on the wooden steps. Once they reached the walkway at the top, Badger raced from one end to the other in a display of victory over the stairs.

Bud examined the nearest door, and a padlock secured it just like the one on the front.

Moving down to the other door, he again became disappointed by the presence of an identical padlock. He peered out over the rail of the walkway. In the yard next door, he saw an elderly lady; she knelt over to prune some flowers in a well-kept bed that ran diagonally from her house.

He quickly trotted back down the stairs with his dog stumbling somewhat all the way down behind him.

"Come on, buddy. You'd better stay in the car. We don't want to give an old lady a fright." Bud walked back to the car and opened the door, gesturing for Badger to get in; reluctantly, he jumped in. Bud quickly closed the door behind him.

As Bud strolled over toward the house next door, he noticed the lady making her way up her front steps.

"Excuse me, madam." Bud hurried to catch her before she went inside. "Excuse me," He raised his voice a bit more this time.

Turning slightly, the lady seemed to hear Bud. Now moving quicker than before, she went to her front door, opened it and stepped inside, shutting it quickly behind her. As Bud made his way up the front steps, he could hear the lock clicking. He stopped midway before reaching the porch.

"Well, I must have frightened her even without Badger," he said softly to himself.

He considered knocking on the door but decided the elderly woman likely didn't want to be disturbed. He turned and gazed across the street from where the apartments stood. There, he saw another large two-story house with a well-kept yard. He jogged across the road to this house.

Badger barked in protest as he passed by the car.

"Yeah, yeah, I know. Hold on just a minute."

He moved quickly up the steps of the porch. There, he found a large screen door painted red, behind which stood a heavy door with a pane of stained glass. The door had the appearance of being quite old. Of the little knowledge he'd gained from his father about these sorts of things, he thought the door may have been produced in the 1930s or 1940s.

He carefully opened the screen door and knocked several times. Soon, footsteps could be heard on the other side of the large door. He then saw movement behind the stained glass. The door opened, and an elderly woman appeared.

"Hello?"

"Hi, I'm sorry to bother you. My name is Bud Fisher, and I'm interested in renting one of the apartments next door. Do you happen to know who owns them?"

The lady examined Bud as if a bit puzzled.

"You want to rent one of the apartments next door?"

"Yes. Please, do you know who owns them?" Bud turned slightly and pointed at the house across the street as he said this.

"Well, no one has lived there for a long time," she replied as she pulled her sweater closed one side at a time. "But I believe the apartments are owned by John Beldon. He owns a number of properties around town, as well as the pharmacy on Main Street."

"Do you know where I could find him?" Bud was desperate to find an alternative sleeping arrangement after his night on the dirt road.

"I believe he might be at the pharmacy. I think it's open today; it's the only pharmacy on Main Street."

"Thank you. Thank you so much. I'll go see if I can catch him before closing time." Bud raced down the steps.

"Well, yes, you're welcome," the lady replied as he trotted across the street to his car.

He located the pharmacy on Main Street with little difficulty. When he saw that the lights on the inside were still on, he almost shouted with joy. Walking to the front door, his main concern became whether the owner of the apartments would be there.

"I'm looking for a John Beldon," he told a cashier with urgency.

"John is the guy with the beard behind the counter," the young woman said, pointing toward the back of the store.

Bud moved briskly to the counter where a heavyset guy with a beard stood working. He wore a white lab coat and appeared to be in his late forties or early fifties.

"Hello, Mr. Beldon?"

"Yes," the man said, turning to Bud. "Can I help you?"

"My name is Bud Fisher, Mr. Beldon. I work with the Cajon Construction Company. We're replacing the insulation on the reciprocators at the paper mill. I'm looking for a rental house or apartment for about four months, maybe three depending on how quickly we finish the job. I saw the apartments on Cooper Lane and heard you would be the one to talk to about renting one of them."

The large man stopped working, and his face went blank. Bud initially thought the elderly woman must have been confused about who owned the apartments. Mr. Beldon began working again.

"Nobody has lived in those apartments for quite some time," he replied, never turning from his work. "I don't know that they would be in any condition to rent."

Bud knew he must work something out, or he would be spending another night in his car.

"Well, I'm not real particular, Mr. Beldon; I just need a roof over my head and the basic necessities. I have cash for rent as well as a little for a deposit right now. I also noticed the yard needed mowing, sir. I would be happy to keep it mowed while I'm there, that is, if you have a mower I could borrow."

When he mentioned mowing the grass, Mr. Beldon stopped working again and glanced up at the potential renter. His demeanor seemed to change.

After what appeared to be some careful thought on his part, John Beldon returned to his work.

"The rooms are furnished, but as I said, no one has lived there for some time, so they likely need a good cleaning. If you keep the yard mowed, I'll only charge you a hundred and seventy-five dollars a month. You can give me fifty for a deposit now and another fifty within the first month."

The young man felt as if a weight had been removed from his shoulders as he heard this.

"Oh, that's great, Mr. Beldon. I really appreciate it."

Mr. Beldon continued, "There's a mower in the storage shed out back. You can use it, but it'll need gas."

After paying his new landlord, Bud got the key to the bottom apartment with the big door. John told him this one appeared to be the best of the four.

Bud stopped by a department store and bought some candles and a flashlight before returning to the apartments. He also had a small AM/FM radio, so he bought some batteries for it. He then stopped at a gas station and filled a few jugs and soda bottles with water. The two then quickly headed back to the apartment to get settled in before dark.

Back at the house, Bud opened the large door, and the long unmoved hinges screeched out of unfamiliarity. He stepped inside, and the pungent smell of a long uninhabited dwelling greeted him.

The evening light shining in through the entrance revealed a spacious living room with a fireplace that had been closed in at some time. A gas heater was instead placed in the area where the log fires had once blazed.

As he slowly continued in, he found a large couch sitting to his right in front of the windows that faced the porch. From the style of the couch, he thought it to be twenty-five or thirty years old. Certainly, it was older than he was. However, it appeared to be in fair shape and didn't have any rips.

In front of him, dividing the living room and bedroom area, stood two large doors with plate glass windows.

Badger remained in the doorway, seeming to wait for his master to give the "all clear" to enter.

"Come on, buddy," he gestured for the dog to enter.

The young man sensed the grandeur of the house as he gazed up to the high ceilings. He walked up to the double doors and opened them both at the same time. A slight breeze flowed past him, and Badger stepped back as if he'd been sprayed with water or had a small rock thrown at him. Chuckling a little, Bud asked, "What's wrong with you, buddy?"

He then moved through the doors and into a bedroom area. There sat a queen-sized bed on his left with a small stand beside it and a lamp on the stand. A single window across from the bed stood open about ten inches or so.

"Well, there's where our breeze is coming from. At least it doesn't smell so stuffy in this room."

The two proceeded to the bedroom area and into the kitchen. To the immediate left, a little hallway led to the bathroom. A large porcelain-covered bathtub with the old ornate legs sat beside a toilet and small sink.

Back in the kitchen, they saw obviously newer cabinets and renovations, reminiscent of when the house was being turned into apartments. Although a little unsightly, the modifications were done well and didn't ruin the original decor of the old structure.

From the kitchen, a back door opened to a small porch on the side of the house. Walking down the porch and around the back, Bud and Badger found themselves underneath the walkway that gave access to the second-story apartments.

As they stood examining the backyard, Bud spoke with a bit of reservation, "I suppose we're going to be camping out with no electricity for a couple nights, boy." He peered down at his friend as if expecting a comment on the matter.

By the time he'd unloaded the car, darkness had set in. He lit some candles, and the light danced off the high ceilings. Bud used some of the water from the jugs to clean up as much as possible. He sat down on the couch and finally relaxed for a few moments. It had been a rough couple of days, but he considered them to be successful, as they now had a place to live.

Monday, he would get the utilities turned on, and then the apartment would be great. He examined the spacious room in the candlelight. This would be comfortable, he thought. The humid night air made everything seem warm and damp. He opened the two large windows behind the couch. As the candlelight burned down and grew weaker, the two became sleepy.

Finally, he got up and headed to the bedroom, blowing out each candle until he extinguished the last one that sat on the headboard of the bed. Badger jumped onto the foot of the bed and lay down. A breeze floated across both from the open windows as they drifted off to sleep.

Sometime later, Badger's sudden movement and low growl brought Bud out of his slumber. The darkness enveloped them both, and he couldn't see much. Initially, he had no idea where he was. Then, as Badger continued to growl with attention toward the window, Bud began to recall moving into the apartment earlier. He strained to see anything familiar through the faint gleam of a distant street light.

He could hear something moving around outside. Badger hadn't moved from his spot at the foot of the bed, but his head remained raised in an alert position as he continued to growl. The dog had been trained not to bark unless necessary.

Bud's mind began to race as his eyes grew accustomed to the darkness. Where did he put the flashlight he'd bought? Did he lock the front door? What could he use as a weapon if he needed to fight?

He quietly slid out of bed and began searching through the small pile of baggage on the bedroom floor. As he did this, Badger hopped off the bed and moved into the living room area, continuing to growl.

Terrified now, Bud crawled around frantically searching for the sack with the flashlight and batteries but had forgotten where he'd put them. He then heard movement on the front porch. One of the old flower pots with dry dirt was knocked over with the distinct sound of clay hitting the porch. Badger's growl became more insistent. He backed up toward his master in apparent apprehension to the unknown nature of the threat outside.

Bud groped around more urgently for anything to use as a weapon. Opening a closet and feeling around on the floor, his hand came across something long just as he could hear the knob on the front door turning. Fear clutched him as he struggled to grasp the object and get up and into a defensive position. Badger's growl became nervous but remained aggressive, as he also sensed the immediate danger.

He lifted what felt to be part of a broom handle from the closet floor, and then stood up as the front door began to open.

Charging toward the entrance, with the broom handle in his right hand, Bud let out a loud yell, or something between a yell and a growl, which came out as, "AARRRRGGGGHHHH."

Badger picked up on his master's intention of an offensive maneuver and began to bark loudly as he joined in the charge beside Bud.

With the sudden attack from Bud and Badger, the intruder was caught by surprise and fell back, kicking the fallen clay pot across the porch while tumbling down the steps to the ground. As Bud and Badger arrived at the open door, a dark figure scampered across the overgrown grass and crashed through the tall hedge, escaping out to the other side.

Closing the door and locking it, he then sat down on the couch, his heart still pounding fiercely. After a few minutes, Bud got up and lit a candle. In a weary state, he'd completely forgotten to lock the front door before going to bed. He must be more diligent from now on, he thought to himself.

After locating the flashlight and installing the batteries, Bud placed it on the headboard and stood the piece of broomstick beside the bed.

"Quite an eventful first night, my friend," he said, looking down at his dog. Slowly, he calmed down enough to fade back to sleep, though not as deeply as earlier.

The next morning, Bud investigated the storage building behind the house. As John had mentioned, inside the shed, he found a push mower and other various yard care tools.

Finding a saw, he put it to use cutting a straight limb from a tree in the back corner of the yard, then fashioned this into a club about the size of a baseball bat.

Bud located a small gas can in the shed. After getting it filled and spending a fair amount of sweat and energy getting the mower started, he mowed the yard little by little, as the grass had become too tall to mow in a normal fashion. Finally, he put the mower up and admired his work. Badger ran about as if possessed by the smell of fresh-cut grass.

After finishing his yard work, Bud went inside and poured the sink in the bathroom full of water, then examined himself in the mirror.

Though only nineteen, he felt that he looked about twenty-one, at least. He also felt older since he had been on his own for a while.

Bud briefly thought of his broken home. He wondered if leaving his parents at such a young age was the right decision. Troubling events such as he'd faced the last several days often caused the young man to question himself.

As usual, though, these wavering feelings inside him only brought anguish. He quickly concluded that he would rather leave than choose between his father and mother. He gazed into the worn ceramic sink and tried to stop thinking about it.

Using a cup, he washed his hair in the old basin and cleaned himself up the best he could. Regardless of the frightening experience of the first night, Bud felt pretty good about his new home.

Chapter Two:

WINDOW OF DISCONTENT

Monday morning, a small group of men were gathered around a picnic table outside the offices of the paper mill. Bud hoped these would be the guys he'd been searching for.

"Is this Cajon Construction?" he asked one of the men.

"Yeah, this is Cajon Construction. I'm Rick Andrews."

Bud extended his hand, "Bud Fisher. Pleased to meet you, Rick."

After being introduced to all the other men, Bud examined the mill a little more closely. Across from where they stood was a large building that appeared to have hefty vats inside as well as assorted machinery. Connected to that building, a structure rose about fifteen to twenty stories high. It wasn't a building so much as a framework holding in place equipment that needed to be elevated.

As he checked out the facility, a white pickup drove up with a Cajon Construction sign on the door. Two men stepped out of the pickup and strolled over to the group. Then, the driver spoke up.

"Hello, guys. Some of you know me, and for those who are new, my name is Roger Corbin. This is your foreman, Don Woods," Roger pointed to the passenger who now stood beside him.

"We're going to get started right away, as we hope to be finished and on our next job in one-hundred-twenty days or less. We're going to start over there," he pointed to the large building. "And we will end, seventeen stories up," he said, pointing to the top of the structure.

"Those of you who are afraid of heights may have problems."

After Roger passed along additional information concerning the job, he left Don in charge, and the crew began their work. Bud received permission to take an extended lunch break to get his utilities turned on.

Later that afternoon, back at the apartments, when Bud opened the front door, Badger bolted out. He ran into the front yard and stood staring back at his master.

"Hey, buddy, what's wrong? You must be tired of being in the house by yourself, huh?" Bud went on in and checked his utilities. It felt good to have the necessities of life again.

Getting Badger back into the house proved challenging, though. Bud thought his dog might sense a bath to be in the near future. After the two received baths and ate dinner, he and Badger both slept well.

The young man took on his new job duties with determination and gusto. However, every afternoon, when Bud got home from work and opened the door, Badger would always bolt out. He began to wonder if his dog may be getting too hot in the apartment.

The following Monday, Bud decided to open the window in the bedroom all the way before leaving for work.

As the day progressed, it developed into a hot one, and Bud realized he'd made the right decision of additional airflow for his canine friend.

When Bud got home, he opened the front door, and Badger once again bolted out. As had become his routine, he ran out into the yard and stared back at Bud as if he'd just escaped from something.

Bud walked into the apartment. It seemed a little warm inside but not unbearable. He moved on into the bedroom to check if a breeze was coming through, then looked at the window and got an eerie surprise. It stood closed down to about ten inches, just as it had been when they moved in.

Badger now walked into the living room and sat down, peering at Bud in something of a puzzled manner.

"Well, for goodness sake, I thought that I'd opened that window for you, boy. Didn't I open that up for you?"

Badger looked at his master and, possibly sensing he wanted an answer, barked at him.

"I guess maybe I closed it back."

He rubbed his head and didn't recall closing it, but thought he must have done so without thinking, before leaving for work.

The following morning, Bud made sure to open the window all the way before leaving.

"There you go, boy. This time, I didn't forget." He glanced at Badger, who watched him with interest.

He left, feeling confident his dog would be more comfortable. It had now become increasingly hotter as summer entrenched itself in the Louisiana town.

The Cajon Company crew busily cleaned the old paint and insulation off the equipment in the large building at ground level. Every day, Bud left work quite dirty and sweaty due to laboring around the large vats. He liked his job, and it paid well for a young man such as him. Oddly, however, as he worked, he noticed the paper mill had a smell of glue. He wasn't sure how to identify the smell, but glue seemed the closest thing he could think of.

That afternoon, he opened the front door, and the same routine played out as usual, with Badger bolting out to the yard.

"Oh, come on now, Badger. It can't be that bad. I opened the window for you." Bud walked into the apartment and sat his lunchbox down on the couch. Badger remained outside, taking care of the bathroom business that he seemed to have been waiting all day to take care of.

Wearily, the young man turned on a box fan in the living room and began shedding his boots one at a time as he moved toward the bathroom.

Once in the bathroom, he began running a bath and then headed back to the bedroom area to retrieve Badger. As he passed by the bed, he glanced across to the window he'd opened that morning. He stopped dead in his tracks and squinted as if he wasn't seeing clearly. He cautiously moved over to the window, which now, once again, stood close to the original ten inches high, as it had been when they moved in.

He examined it with apprehension. Where the lock should have been, he could see an outline, as if a lock had been there at one time but was removed. He then opened the window and tried closing it again, thinking it may be sliding down from its own weight. The pressure to close it, however, was more than it would take to shut on its own. Several times, he opened the window and closed it, testing the effort required. He reluctantly returned to his mission of getting his dog back into the house.

After fetching Badger, he again went to the window; the strange occurrence now clung to his mind. He studied it from every angle and became so intent upon solving the mystery that he completely forgot about his bathwater. Bud ran into the bathroom to find the tub full and only inches from running over the top. He quickly turned the water off and resumed his previous plan of getting cleaned up. Afterward, the window became somewhat diminished in his thoughts as he ate dinner and prepared for bed.

The following morning, Bud opened the window all the way once again. As the day went by, he occasionally wondered about it. That afternoon, when he opened the front door, Badger again expressed an extreme eagerness to get out of the apartment. This time, Bud went straight to the window and again found it open at about ten inches. The young man struggled with this unusual situation later as he sat on the aged couch, eating dinner.

For the remainder of the week, Bud checked the window, and every day that week, the window would somehow be closed to ten inches, though he'd opened it all the way before leaving.

That weekend, he bought a run line for Badger and ran it along the back of the house and to the storage building. The dog appeared much more content when Bud got home from work the following Monday.

After resolving the issue with Badger, he became less concerned about the window. He left it open at its stubborn ten-inch gap and more-or-less forgot the situation for the time being, rationalizing the strange occurrence to it being an old house.

As the days grew warmer, the crew moved from the large building into the tall structure that housed equipment and machinery, which the paper mill used for processing purposes. At the top, which turned out to be seventeen stories high, sat the reciprocator that they would be working on last. Slowly, day by day, they moved up the structure. As part of the crew removed the old paint and insulation, another part repainted and re-insulated on the opposite side. After about six weeks, they were halfway up. At this point, the work became increasingly dangerous due to the height. Some areas required the crew to build scaffolding along the outside of the structure to get the work completed.

On one particular day, it had become very hot by the time Bud reached the apartment. He let Badger off the run line and headed inside. After cleaning up and eating, he laid down.

The fan in the living room had worked well so far, but now during the hottest part of the summer, the air seemed to hang damply all around him rather than move over him and cool him down. He didn't want the fan blowing directly on him, so he opened the window beside the bed and then lay back down and went to sleep.

When Bud awoke in the morning, he became a bit startled to find the window had closed during the night to the ten inches.

"Well, if that isn't the strangest thing," he said to himself and partly to his canine friend. "I'm not quite sure what to do about that." He walked over to it, and in one motion, he took hold of the window and pushed it closed. "Now, that's the end of that," he said, looking down to Badger with satisfaction. His dog replied with a whine.

Again, the crew moved up a floor. The view became intoxicating as well as frightening. There were no walls on the structure, just rails along the edge. The functions of the paper mill gave distinct sounds of vapor moving inside pressurized pipes and running diagonally up and down the seventeen-story structure.

The summer breeze felt warm but stirred enough to relieve some of the men's distress. As the day went by, Bud would joke around with the guys.

There happened to be one crew member who Bud got along with exceptionally well. His name was Donnie, and the two worked side by side on many occasions, becoming good friends in the process. By the time the job was half-finished, they would be keeping each other entertained with humorous remarks and witty observations.

"Hey, you better be sure your safety harness is hooked up," Donnie said as Bud prepared to go to the scaffolding.

Bud looked at Donnie, a bit puzzled. "Do you really think I should?"

After leaning a little to peer over the long drop to the ground, Donnie replied rather casually. "Well, you don't have to if you don't want to. But if you fall, I'm sure not cleaning up the mess!"

Bud laughed. "You wouldn't? And I thought you were my friend."

Donnie chuckled, and Bud continued.

"Yeah, I'll be sure to hook the safety line up. I'd look like a bug on a windshield after a fall like that." He then began putting his safety harness on.

Later that day, he arrived home and went around to the back. Badger, as usual, was excited to see his master.

"Hey, boy, how did your day go?" Badger sat down and barked a short staccato at Bud. "Yeah, yeah, I know. Ready to get off this line, eh?"

They walked back around to the front of the house and up the steps. Bud unlocked the door and walked inside. Badger, however, sat down outside the doorway.

"Come on, buddy. I'm ready to get cleaned up and eat something."

Badger got up and walked around in a circle, and then he sat back down and whined. Bud stared curiously at his dog, trying to figure out what the problem could be.

"What's going on, Badger? Stop messing around and get in here. I told you I'm tired."

Badger stood up and gently walked through the front doorway as if moving on a slick surface. The young man laughed at this sight and closed the door behind him once the dog had cautiously made his way in.

Bud turned on the box fan in the living room and once again glanced down at his dog, which was standing as if reluctant to move.

"You're sure acting nutty today."

The sound of the fan muffled his remarks as he moved on to the bedroom and then the kitchen.

After placing his lunchbox on the cabinet, he walked back into the bedroom and, facing the bed, pulled his tee-shirt up over his head. As the shirt cleared his eyes, he looked straight at the window. He stopped at that point, before getting the shirt completely off. The window he had shut that morning was now open to its usual spot about ten inches high.

Bud's eyes became fixed on the unexpected sight. He slowly moved over to the window, pulling his shirt the rest of the way off and tossing it onto the bed. He examined the window as if it were an ill pet. He got down on his knees and ran his finger along the points where the frames mated together. Then, he examined the inside of the frame on both sides. He stood up and then stepped back, staring at it with confusion.

"What's going on here?"

He turned back to where Badger would generally be, but the dog still stood in the living room, at the same spot he'd assumed earlier. Bud walked to the double doors and looked at his dog. He now sensed something very strange was going on in the house.

"Come on, boy. It's all right."

Badger walked cautiously over to his master. After Bud petted and reassured the dog, he relaxed a bit. The young man got cleaned up and prepared his meal. He sat on the couch, eating dinner, and considering the situation with the window. Finally, he turned to Badger lying at his feet and, as if suddenly solving a problem, said, "I know what we're going to do."

Badger raised his head and gave a general response, a low whine.

The next morning, before taking Badger to the run line, Bud went to the window. He took a pen and marked where it was opened to.

"First, we'll make sure something odd is actually going on here and eliminate any other possible explanations." He then shut the window. As an extra measure, he gave it a firm press downward before taking Badger out back and leaving for work.

The seventeenth floor now loomed overhead in silent anticipation for the crew. A daily routine developed from repeating their tasks, and likewise, the job progressed more rapidly. The efficiency from this routine also convinced everyone they would finish the job ahead of schedule. Bud gazed out over the town and took a deep breath. At this height, the air smelled fresh, and a constant breeze blew, keeping him cooler than when the work had been at lower levels.

"We'll be on top next week," Donnie said as he walked up to Bud.

"Yeah, that'll be something." Bud glanced back at his friend. The two walked back to the rest of the crew and prepared everything for the day's work. He now had some extra money saved and felt good about his overall situation.

Bud pulled into the drive of the big house that afternoon. Before getting out of the car, he examined the old building closely. It presented a starkly different appearance to him lately. Rather than a set of ordinary apartments, he now saw an old mansion with a long history that he knew nothing about. He studied the large front porch and tried to imagine people from fifty years ago walking up and down the steps. He got out of the car and went back to get Badger. His canine friend sat on the green grass, and as Bud walked up, the dog growled at him, seeming unsure who approached him.

"Hey, buddy, what's up with you?"

Badger stared at his master, and as if the sound of his voice were a key, the dog immediately jumped up and started wagging his stubby tail.

"Has there been someone else around here?" Bud asked and glanced around, wondering about his dog's strange behavior.

When they got to the front door, Badger once again didn't want to go inside until his master insisted. Bud then walked to the window. It was up again.

"Well, well," he said, walking over for a closer look.

He examined the window and the mark he'd placed on it that morning. The marks almost mated up perfectly. He looked around as if searching for someone. Bud's hair began to tingle as invisible fingers seemed to take hold on the back of his neck and then crawled over his head. He stood up quickly and moved to the other side of the bed to get away from the frightening presence. The silence of the room now felt thick all around him. There was some type of force close by; he sensed it, and Badger did too.

Badger let out a low aggressive growl. Bud searched the room in vain for some sign of what he felt was there and what Badger was now acting defensive about.

He moved with fear in his steps to the living room, attempting to get away from the unseen entity. Badger followed him until he got to the double doors; then, the dog stopped suddenly. He now stared ominously into the living room where Bud stood, and then began to growl again.

"Is it in here with me?" Bud stared back at his dog for a clue to the unseen presence.

Badger appeared not to hear Bud. Instead, he continued to growl and stare at something beside his master. Bud now felt the unnatural force moving in the room, and panic clenched his being as he realized whatever it was that had been existing in the house with them was now directly beside him. Another chill shot through him, and fear gripped his insides as Badger continued in his defensive behavior.

Seeming to have few options other than fleeing in fright or somehow fighting the force, Bud took an entirely offensive stance that even surprised him. In an act of anger at not being able to see what threatened him, he suddenly shouted, "I'm not leaving this house. Do you hear me?"

Then, after a few seconds of eerie silence, Badger slowly walked into the living room, inspecting the entire area as if trying to identify what had been there. Bud watched his canine companion as he attempted to calm down from the incident.

He still felt angry as he stood frozen and seemingly defenseless in the room. He wanted to do something, so he went to the kitchen and looked in one of the drawers. He found some nails and then went out to his car and retrieved the hammer he used at work. Still worked up over the incident, he went to the window, slammed it shut, and placed a nail above the frame. He then nailed it in far enough that the window could not open.

"There you go," he said in a loud voice. "Open the window now! This may have been your house at one time, but it's my house now. Do you hear me?"

He then sat on the bed and laid the hammer down as he would a weapon. Bud felt tired and hungry, and wanted to get clean. He turned to Badger. "We showed 'em, didn't we boy?"

It felt to be a hollow victory. He now knew they weren't alone, and that was very frightening. He tried not to think about it and decided to return to his routine.

After getting cleaned up and eating, Bud sat on the bed again. The day's events had exhausted him, but he didn't really want to turn the lights off. After a few moments, he got up and walked through the door to the kitchen and took an immediate left to the short hallway to the bathroom. He turned on the bathroom light and closed the door almost all the way. He went back to the bedroom, turned off the light and sat down.

The light that came through the cracked bathroom door lit up the kitchen and bedroom like a nightlight would. He felt a little better now. Should he be confronted by something, hopefully, he would be able to at least see what he would be fighting. He crawled into bed and slowly drifted off to sleep.

The next day was Friday. At the morning safety meeting, Don told everyone the crew would be on the top next week and would finish the job quickly once there. He also said plans were being made to move the crew to the next job site. Bud now felt eager to finish the job. He'd become determined not to move from the apartment, but the recent events were becoming more and more troubling.

As the day wore on, he decided that helped him resolve the turmoil in his mind. He decided that if he wasn't physically threatened by the invisible specter in the house, he wouldn't leave. However, if this ghost or whatever it was, showed an ability to harm him physically, then he would get out.

The pact he made with himself caused instant relief to the turmoil in his mind. Now, he had a plan, and he thought this to be reasonable. Why should he leave if there wasn't a real threat to his general well-being? By the end of the day, he felt revamped and ready to resist the entity in his apartment.

Chapter Three:

THE UNSEEN STAIRS

After work, the same day, Bud pulled into the drive. The large house loomed over him as he walked to the backyard. Badger again acted apprehensive as his master approached. He unhooked the dog from the run line, and they strolled around to the front steps together. Bud sat down on the steps and had Badger sit in front of him.

"All right, buddy," he took hold of Badger's muzzle shaking it a little as he would do at times. "Here's the deal. I know why you've been acting so strangely. I'm sorry if I was a little rough on you. I'm not sure what you've been seeing during the day, but I suspect it's the same thing we confronted last night."

Badger stared intently at his master, as if he understood some of what Bud was telling him.

"I've decided that we're going to stay here until the job is finished, as long as whatever it is we're up against isn't able to harm either one of us. I think it's just trying to scare us off. I'm not going to scare off that easy though, what about you?"

Badger sneezed.

"I guess I'll take that as a definite maybe," Bud replied.

He then walked into the apartment with Badger following cautiously behind him. As had slowly become a routine for Badger, he sniffed around the living room for something unseen in the house. Bud tried to sense a foreign presence but now decided the best method would be to watch Badger's actions.

After investigating the living room, the dog strolled through the double doors into the bedroom, still searching for a trace of the invisible intruder. He then went into the kitchen and bathroom area and, shortly after, trotted back into the living room where Bud stood.

"I guess we've swapped places, eh boy? Now, I'm the one standing by a door." Bud placed his lunchbox on the couch and walked toward the bedroom.

As Bud entered the bedroom, he glanced over at the window and noticing it remained closed. Smiling with satisfaction, he moved closer to the window, and the smile quickly fell from his face.

The nail he had driven in above the frame was bent upward, indicating a force pushing up on the window. It stood clearly ten feet from the ground and inaccessible from the outside without a ladder. Bud now felt the chill crawl up his back again. He touched the nail, seeming to want proof that it was made of steel.

Moving away from the window, he pushed the feeling of terror back down, remaining determined to stick to his plan.

The day ended as Bud sat down to eat. The apartment displayed an ominous appearance now that he'd never noticed before. Once again, he turned the light on in the bathroom and closed the door leaving a small crack as he had done the night before. The kitchen and the bedroom were lit up well through the short hallway behind his bed.

Bud lay down and stared at the ceiling. He noticed the color to be a yellowish tan in the dim light. This seemed to be a warm color and had a comforting feel. The thought caused a calming effect, and he easily slipped into sleep.

A sudden movement from Badger jolted Bud out of his slumber. Looking straight up at the ceiling, he became paralyzed by what he saw. Shadows were dancing on the ceiling. He watched as distinct outlines of people moved about as if they were in the bathroom hallway and kitchen.

The young man slowly looked down at the foot of the bed where Badger was. The dog's head was lifted as if also having been surprised. Badger stared alertly at the shadows. Bud now realized the reflections were also moving on the wall across from the bed. The sight of his dog sitting this way, at the foot of the bed, cast an odd and surreal image to him.

Next, he wondered why his dog wasn't barking or at least growling. He wanted him to growl, or bark or anything to chase away the specters. For a moment, he watched Badger sitting and studying the shadows. His fear turned to anger at his dog.

As he continued to wake up, though, he became aware of something he'd not noticed in his drowsy state, and it slowly dawned on him why Badger neglected to bark or even growl. No sounds were accompanying the shadows.

Badger watched them with keen interest, in the way a young boy might watch a large bug crawl along the ground. Bud slowly and carefully sat up in bed. Badger paid him little attention. The young man also watched the shadows and, after a few minutes, became not so much afraid as perplexed by the sheer strangeness of it.

Just as the two were becoming very interested in the shadows, the situation changed. The distinct sound of a person walking issued from upstairs. It came from behind the wall where the strange shadows reflected. Then, on across the floor, the footsteps moved over them with distinguishable sounds of creaking boards. Badger looked up at the ceiling and began to growl in a low steady tone. Bud's hair again began to crawl along his neck as curiosity quickly transformed into an almost paralyzing fear.

Sliding out of bed, Bud picked up the club he'd placed beside it. Badger also bounced off and trotted into the living room, then back into the bedroom, growling along the way. The footsteps continued to move around on the second floor above them. They were heavy and slow, like those of a large man.

The footsteps then moved back down the mysterious stairs behind the wall. From the sound, they seemed to enter the kitchen. Bud moved slowly toward the door with the club raised. He peeked around the corner into the kitchen and hallway. There was no one there, and the shadows evaporated.

Backing up, he turned his attention to his dog, which now stood in apparent confusion as well.

Suddenly, the footsteps moved rapidly back up the ghostly stairs behind the wall. They ran over the top of the living room area and faded into the other side of the house.

Becoming excited by the unexpected movement, Badger chased the footsteps into the living room and to the old fireplace, at which point he could follow them no longer and barked as if he'd been the one to frighten them away.

After this event, Bud remained awake for a while. He got a snack and turned the radio on. Sitting on the couch, he peered into the kitchen, watchful for any new evidence of the shadows on the wall. An uneventful hour passed, and he went back to bed, finally falling asleep again.

The following morning, Bud and Badger ate breakfast as usual on his Saturdays. He then went outside to the front porch and walked down to the door on the other end. The lock remained secure, and there was no evidence that it had been open for some time.

Moving around to the back of the house, he jogged up the steps leading to the two upstairs apartments. He carefully examined both locks, and as with the front door, these were also secure and undisturbed. He went down the stairs and moved around the house, inspecting for other possible entry points.

After a thorough review of the house, and finding no evidence of any intruders, Bud decided to get on with the day's activities. He loaded his laundry in the Pontiac and put Badger on the run line.

The first stop would be the drug store on Main Street, to pay Mr. Beldon for another week's rent and to let him know his crew would likely be finished soon.

Passing through the aisles with shoe insoles, Band-aids and various stomach remedies, Bud could see John Beldon at the back of the store working. Mr. Beldon stood behind the counter filling prescriptions, as he always seemed to be doing when Bud came to talk with him. He waited patiently with the rent in hand. After a few moments, Mr. Beldon turned his attention to Bud.

"Hello, can I help you?"

"Mr. Beldon, I just came to give you one more week's rent. My crew will be finishing up next week." Bud held the money up for him.

"Oh, well, all right," Mr. Beldon replied as he finished a prescription. "Give me just a minute, would you?" He continued his work.

"Yes, sir." Bud moved down the counter a bit, looking over some ingrown toenail medicine that he was quite certain he didn't need.

"Okay, so you just want to pay one more week's rent, you said?" John put a label on a medicine bottle and now gave Bud his full attention.

"Yes, sir. We'll be finishing up next week."

Mr. Beldon pulled a receipt book from a drawer under his counter. "I noticed you've been keeping the yard cut well. Everything else been going all right?" He began writing out the receipt.

Bud felt a strong desire to tell him everything that had happened recently. Then, that urge was tempered by a question in his mind; had Mr. Beldon had heard any stories from previous renters?

The young man struggled with what to say. This long pause aroused Mr. Beldon's attention. He stopped writing and turned to Bud in anticipation of an answer.

"Well, umm," Bud stammered a bit to end the silence as he grasped for something to say. "I think there may be someone getting into the upstairs apartments somehow."

Mr. Beldon's face became serious now, but Bud noticed he didn't appear to be surprised.

"What do you mean?" he asked as he glanced back down at the receipt and then continued to write.

"I heard footsteps above my room last night. I don't know how they could be getting into the upstairs apartments; the locks seem to be secure and unopened."

"Are you sure it was footsteps you heard? That's an old house, you know," Mr. Beldon asked this as he gazed over the receipt to check it for correctness.

"Yes, sir, I'm sure I heard footsteps."

John tore the receipt from the booklet, and Bud handed the money to him. He didn't hand the receipt to Bud, though; instead, he stared at the paper in one hand and held the money in the other, as if trying to decide.

After a few seconds, he sat the receipt back down on the counter in front of him. He looked at Bud and breathed deeply as if he'd decided on something but wanted to determine the best way to present it. He then reached into his pocket and pulled out some keys and began separating one from the ring.

"Ordinarily, I wouldn't do something like this. But you've been a good renter, and I don't have the time right now to address the situation."

Once the key became separated from the others, he glanced at it and then briefly to Bud. "I happened to notice you have a large dog in the backyard."

"Yes, sir," Bud replied, not sure yet what he might be getting at. Mr. Beldon handed the key to him and then picked up the receipt and handed it to him. He then looked at Bud again. The young man noticed Mr. Beldon had the same look he did a few months earlier when he'd mentioned mowing the yard.

"That key fits all the other apartment doors. I realize you probably don't have a phone to call the police, but if you hear anything else and want to take your dog up and have a look, you're welcome to do so. The only other option would be to drive to the police station, I suppose. Either way, you have the key now, and if you have any more trouble, you can deal with it as you deem best."

Mr. Beldon picked up another paper that appeared to be a prescription and began to work on it.

"I'll be out of town for a few weeks starting next week, so when you leave, just drop the keys off with Nancy upfront. If you happen to need more time, she can take the rent and give you a receipt." Once again, he stopped his work and turned to Bud as if assuring himself of making the right decision.

"Okay, I'll do that, sir, and thank you." Bud then put the key and receipt in his pocket.

"You're welcome," John said and returned to the work in front of him.

It was late afternoon when Bud finished his laundry and his shopping and returned to the apartment. He let Badger off the line, then went inside and sat on the couch. He pulled the key from his pocket and sat it on the coffee table. He stared at the brass key for several minutes, as if it would reveal some answer to a question he had on his mind.

He thought of going straight up the stairs and to the room over his. He wanted to, and even imagined himself putting the key in the lock and opening the door. Then, everything grew cloudy in his mind, and again, the key came into view. He'd never considered this possible turn of events.

The young man examined this new thing sitting on the coffee table; this small key on the table had suddenly changed the situation. His manhood almost felt threatened by this tiny brass key. Why not go straight up the stairs and see what was up there? He struggled with this question for a few moments. Before, he had no option to investigate the strange occurrences. Now, the path was clear. Was he too afraid?

Badger sat on the other side of the coffee table, staring at his master.

"It's a clever thing for Mr. Beldon to give me the key," he said, gazing down at Badger. "He knows; surely he knows the situation," Bud continued, half thinking aloud and half talking to Badger. "He wants us to go confront whatever it is up there, so he won't have to. I'll bet he wants you and me to do it because he thinks a dog may be able to run whatever it is off."

The dog simply stared attentively at Bud and then made a choking, barking sound that he tended to make when he had trouble understanding Bud.

"If you and I confront it, then perhaps 'it' will leave, and he can rent the apartments again. That is the move of a shrewd businessman for you."

Bud grew tired as he pondered the underlying reasoning of him now having access to the rest of the house. He laid his head back on the couch and drifted off to sleep.

Chapter Four:

FORBIDDEN ROOM

A woman screamed somewhere above Bud. Opening his eyes, he looked straight up at the ceiling of the living room. The creaking of ancient floorboards above him indicated someone walking fast toward the direction of the scream. The footsteps followed the same path as before and faded off past the old fireplace.

Bud struggled to wake up. Badger ran around the living room, growling upward at the sounds above. Bud stood up, still gazing at the ceiling; he started toward the bedroom to get his club but stopped in his tracks before taking another step. The double doors to the bedroom were closed. He didn't close them; he was sure he didn't.

Fear crept up the back of his spine with a cold chill. His hair tingled. He rubbed the back of his neck, trying to make it quit. He walked to the doors and attempted to open them. They wouldn't open. He looked through the glass windows and seeing his club beside the bed, he quickly considered breaking the glass as he paced around the living room, still rubbing the back of his neck. Someone must be in trouble; a woman must be in danger upstairs. Or was it his imagination? The doors certainly weren't. He should do something. The young man couldn't relax as he felt the need to act immediately. There may be no time to seek help.

Bud grabbed the car keys and the key to the other rooms from the coffee table and jogged out the front door. He opened the trunk of his car and rummaged around for a flashlight. Locating an old one, he turned it on. The light worked, but not very well. Badger stood close, right next to his leg. The young man dug around some more and found a tire iron. Swinging it a little to get a feel for how it handled, he quickly started around to the back of the house.

The darkness was stifling as Bud moved with caution along the side of the large gloomy old house. The flashlight emitted a weak light, but it didn't falter. Bud chided himself in a low voice for not having a better flashlight in the trunk. The steps came into view and appeared threatening in the darkness. He shined the light up the stairs and briefly hesitated.

Taking a deep breath, he glanced down at Badger in an effort to reassure himself of not being alone. He braced himself and slowly made his way up the stairs. His legs felt heavy; sweat trickled down the side of his face. He wiped the sweat off with his right shoulder and looked back. Badger was cautiously following him as he'd hoped. The door now came into view. Shining the light on the entryway, he found the lock was still in place.

Perhaps Mr. Beldon gave him the wrong key. He was almost hopeful that the key wouldn't work. Bud pulled the small brass key from his pocket and realized his hand was trembling. He slid it into the lock and felt the grooves moving against the tumblers. Turning the key slowly, the lock clicked open. The sound seemed like glass breaking in the night.

There was no sound. Bud became keenly aware of the unsettling silence. He gazed out over the rail, seeing only a single distant streetlight.

As he opened the door, Bud immediately began shining the dim light in. He could smell the old furniture and carpet; the smoke from cigarettes and cigars long extinguished; all blended into a single distinct aroma after being closed in and locked up for far too long. He cautiously stepped into the dark room, raising the tire iron to a ready position.

Directly inside the apartment, he found himself in a small kitchen area. To the right, were a sink and counter. As he moved farther into the room, dust particles floated in front of the dim flashlight. Straining to see into the apartment, Bud managed to make out a living room area. Past this, he could see what appeared to be a bathroom, built when the house was made into apartments. He continued slowly to the edge of the living room.

Farther ahead, a closed door came into view. A faded pink couch covered with the typical sixties-style furniture cloth sat against the wall on the left side. A wooden coffee table with skinny legs that also appeared to hail from the nineteen sixties sat in front of the couch. On the right were several corner tables with lamps on them.

The room appeared to be waiting for someone to come in and turn the lights on, throw their keys on the coffee table and sit down for a relaxing evening. The strange sensation of being in someone's house without their permission settled uneasily on the young man as he stood in the darkness. He moved slowly over to one of the lamps and turned the switch in a vain hope that it might light up. But the clicking sound failed to produce light; it only pierced the silence of the vacant room, as if reminding Bud, he was the intruder in this place.

He moved across the room to the closed door. From sheer force of habit, Bud considered knocking on the door. Before his hand raised, though, he stopped and, realizing how ridiculous the gesture would be in this situation, shook his hand a little to rid him of any more silliness. Reaching out to the doorknob, he clasped it gently as if taking hold of something that might be hot. He turned the knob and opened the door, squeezing the flashlight in as soon as he could.

Inside the dimly lit room and beside a wall sat a large bed with only an uncovered and well-worn mattress on it. An old iron rail frame of the forties or fifties held the box springs in place. A weathered wooden chest of drawers stood against the opposing wall. Bud shined the light down to the wooden claw legs on the old set of drawers. He hadn't seen this type of furniture since he was a young boy visiting his grandmother. Moving the light, he saw the windows were covered with heavy curtains that completely blocked any sign of the outdoors behind them. They appeared to have been a cream color at one time, but after years of neglect, had taken on a yellow shade.

He now went a little farther into the bedroom. It resembled something caught in a time trap. Although apprehensive, the novelty of this room had him slightly distracted.

Unexpectedly, a noise that sounded like a door slamming came from the next apartment over. Badger began growling again but didn't venture from behind Bud. Fright once again tried to paralyze the young man as he turned around. He raised the tire iron in a defensive gesture and then shined the dim flashlight back into the living room but didn't see anyone else in the apartment.

Retracing their steps, the two made it back to the walkway. After locking the door again, they moved down to the adjacent apartment. The experience of investigating the previous rooms now tempered Bud to the fear of checking this one. He once again inserted the key into the lock, and once again, this lock snapped open. He wiped the sweat from his forehead before opening the door. Again, he slowly opened the door and shined the weak flashlight in as soon as he could squeeze through the opening.

There was no odor of a closed-up building this time. Instead, the air smelled fresh, though he detected a faint odor of burned wood. Walking through the door, the sound of something tipping over or falling off a table in the room ahead greeted Bud. Badger followed his master in for a few steps, but when the sound confronted them, Bud noticed Badger began backing out of the doorway.

"Hey, where do you think you're going?" Badger moaned and moved out to the walkway then sat down. "Aren't you coming?" Bud asked in a whispered voice. Badger moaned as if he had an upset stomach.

"Are you kidding me? You're not sick. Don't give me that."

Badger whined and growled at the same time, then laid down, putting his head on his paws.

"I don't believe it," Bud said, shaking his head and then turning back toward the foreboding apartment.

The kitchen in this apartment sat in the same general location as the one next door. As he stood in this area, shining the light in front of him, Bud could also see a built-in bathroom between the kitchen and living room area. Past that area, he saw what appeared to be a bedroom. The door to this room was cracked open.

He moved through the kitchen slowly, holding the flashlight in his left hand and the tire iron in a cocked position in his right. When he reached the living room area, he could see an old couch against the wall on his right. On his left sat several tables with lamps on them. The windows in this apartment were also covered by heavy curtains.

A sudden movement in the room ahead gave Bud another shock. As he stood beside the kitchen sink, something or someone moved in the bedroom; a noise as if a small item had fallen on the floor issued from the room. Bud took a quick breath of air and felt like running back out the door. Instead, he stood frozen with the dim light shining on the bedroom door. He thought he saw movement inside along with an odd noise.

Bud tried to move forward, but his heart was beating so fast he felt he might faint if he took a step. He wanted to look back to see if Badger may have decided to follow him, but he'd lost the ability to do anything other than stare at the ominous door, waiting for the unknown entity to move again. There was a strange sensation he would suddenly see someone, or something quickly walk out the door and straight toward him. Finally, after what felt like an eternity, Bud's heart began to beat slower. He again wiped the sweat from his forehead.

Turning to look behind him, he realized how thick the darkness had become around him. He turned the flashlight around far enough to see Badger still lying at the door with his head cocked up, alertly watching his master.

In a hushed voice, Bud spoke, "Are you going to help me if something's in here?"

Badger moaned and gave the familiar, quick coughing bark, suggesting he wasn't sure what his master said. Bud's face curled in disappointment. Then, realizing his canine friend likely couldn't see his face, he added an "uh-huh" to be certain Badger understood his disappointment.

Once again, he turned back toward the bedroom door. He cautiously moved step by step toward it. The smell of burned wood became more distinct as he got closer.

The bedroom appeared to be dark inside, even with the light shining through the slight crack of the doorway. Bud came right up to it and shined the light in at every angle possible, moving his head up and down a little and then side to side, cautiously trying to get a better view of the inside. He pushed the door open with his fingertips. Blackness and the odor of burned wood and furniture moved around Bud as he stood, nervously gazing in.

The room, the bed and the furniture; all were burned and black. He shined the light from one side to the other. Oddly, only the inside of the room had burned. Somehow, the fire didn't move past the bedroom. Beside the windows, he could see some of the old framework and the blackened glass. There was unburned wood exposed around the windows where the frames and windows had been removed.

It seemed that after the fire, someone had begun to repair the damage, but only got as far as pulling out the old window frames on the inside before abandoning the work. The screens were still in place, and this was why, if standing outside looking up at the room, he could not see that it had burned. A breeze flowed in through the glassless windows. This moved the smell of the burned room all around him.

As he stood in the door, he had a strange feeling about this room, though it wasn't frightening. He searched in his mind for the appropriate description. Then, it came to him rather suddenly and weighed heavily upon him. He wanted to leave.

With caution, Bud backed out of the door. He moved toward where Badger lay. He got to the kitchen area; behind him, he heard a door being slammed shut. Heavy footsteps were walking quickly toward him. He tried to move fast, but fear slowed his effort. Before he could turn, the footsteps sounded as if they walked straight into the wall of the living room to his left.

As he turned completely around to confront the threat, the footsteps moved heavily downstairs on the other side of the wall. They faded away as they got to the point that would be in the apartment downstairs and directly underneath him.

With a trembling hand, he pointed the dim flashlight to examine the bedroom door again. The door stood opened slightly just as it was when he saw it the first time. He crept cautiously back into the living room area, then thought his heart might pop out of his chest, as it now labored inside him.

He closely examined the areas where he heard the sounds. The wall moving along the kitchen area angled abruptly, and there was about a six-foot section of wall in the living room that didn't appear to belong there. The wall looked to be farther inside this apartment than it should be based on where the adjacent apartment door stood. From the strange renovations, Bud determined a section behind the kitchen wall had been blocked off when the house was made into apartments.

After the hasty examination of the wall where the footsteps had faded into, Bud moved back out of the apartment. A weight lifted from his mind when he reached the walkway where Badger still laid waiting for his master. Bud locked the door and then turned to Badger.

"All right then, let's go, Bambi."

The large Doberman moaned in objection, indicating he was aware his master was chastising him.

"Hey, you left me hanging back there, buddy. What do you expect?"

They moved down the stairs quickly, and Bud felt relieved to be getting some distance between him and the disturbing apartment.

Strolling around the front of the house and up the steps, Bud knew he must find out about the mysterious section of wall he'd discovered upstairs. As they got up the steps, Badger headed straight for their apartment door. However, Bud went to the empty downstairs apartment doorway. Badger stopped and looked at him as if questioning where he was going. Bud stared at Badger defiantly.

"I'm going in this apartment. Are you going with me, or are you a big chicken?"

Badger lowered his head and trotted over to Bud, obviously desiring to redeem himself.

Unlocking the apartment next to his, Bud carefully opened the door. The now-familiar smell of a house that had been closed for too long once again greeted him. He shined the light into the apartment and slowly stepped inside. Badger put his nose in the doorway to investigate the room first by smell.

The living room was set up like Bud's apartment. The ceilings were high, and an old couch and coffee table sat to his right and in front of the windows facing the porch. The couch appeared to be covered with the old vinyl that you always stuck to when hot and sweaty. The coffee table resembled the ones Bud remembered from the early 1970s. The carpet was medium shag and an awful shade of green.

As he investigated the apartment, the silence hovered around them, and every little movement reverberated throughout the hushed room. He and Badger ventured farther into the apartment; he noticed what appeared to be a closet of some sort on the wall to his left. From the angle running along the top, Bud knew this closet had been built underneath a stairway.

He opened the door and shined the light in to make sure there were stairs still hidden. The top of the closet ran from the ceiling all the way down to the floor at the opposite end.

"This is where the stairs that lead to the second floor used to be," he said quietly to Badger. His dog subtly moaned a confirmation to his master as he moved around the living room, still inspecting the apartment with his sense of smell.

Bud walked along the wall and followed it into the kitchen area. The wall took a sudden left, and there he saw a nook built into the area where the stairs would start. Inside the nook sat a small metal dining table with two chairs that matched the table. These were visibly old pieces of furniture with metal frames and plastic covered cushions.

Holding the dim light in the nook, he examined it at different angles.

"The stairs are still closed up inside there."

His dog peered curiously into the area, trying to determine what his master had found so interesting.

"At least we know where the stairs are now. A person might think he's losing his mind hearing footsteps on stairs if there are no stairs."

Although the find was comforting in some respect, it didn't resolve the mystery. Now, he wondered whom the footsteps could belong to, why they were going up and down the stairs.

The two cautiously moved back out of the apartment and onto the front porch. Then, after relocking the door, they walked back down to their apartment. They both eagerly entered the doorway, where the living room light shined.

Bud checked the double doors again, finding them locked just as before. "I think we may have to break in. I'm sure I locked the back door from the inside."

Badger lay down on the carpet, and Bud also felt the events of the night weighing on him.

"Or, I guess we can try to pick the lock," he said to Badger. The dog made no effort to get up but rather tucked his head farther into his curled-up body.

"I suppose we might have better luck tomorrow, after some rest." Bud took his jacket and used it as a blanket as he laid down on the couch. Very briefly, he thought he might have trouble sleeping, but after only a few moments, he fell fast asleep.

In the morning, Bud was woken by the sound of a horn honking outside. He rose and glanced out the open window to see Donnie from work sitting in his pickup. Badger barked a little due to the sudden noise.

"It's all right, boy."

He got up and stretched from the turbulent night as he walked outside. Rubbing the sleep from his eyes, he made his way to Donnie's pickup, which sat along the side of the road but pulled up sideways to the drive, far enough to be out of the roadway. His driver's side faced the apartments.

"Hey, buddy, you're not an easy person to find," Donnie said cheerfully, and before Bud could say anything, Donnie continued. "And I can see why; man, what a setup." Donnie examined the big house quickly and once again continued. "You got this whole house to yourself?"

"No, just one apartment," Bud replied, pointing at the sign that was still half-covered by the bush.

"Well, still, this looks a lot better than a motel room." Donnie then seemed to remember why he was there.

"Anyway, the reason I came by is to let you know that you, Jerry and a couple others from the crew are to go over to Reston the day after tomorrow to help another crew finish up there."

"What are you talking about?" Bud stared at Donnie in obvious confusion. He still didn't feel awake yet.

"Yeah, Roger has been looking for you. He talked to me yesterday afternoon, and all I could remember was you saying your place was on Cooper Lane. I would've driven right past it if not for your Pontiac sitting out front."

Bud stood bewildered beside the truck for a few seconds, thinking. After some thought, he replied with a bit of frustration, "I've already paid for this week's rent."

"Well, that's why Roger is giving you guys tomorrow off, so you can get any loose ends tied up. If you can't get a refund on your rent, then I'd tell Roger. Who knows? He might help you out under the circumstances."

After thinking about this, Bud replied softly, "Yeah, I guess so."

"Hey, you want me to take your group toolbox key to Roger. It'll save you a trip in tomorrow. If you don't get that turned in before the job is finished, the paper mill will charge you for it, and I hear it's not cheap."

"Yeah, that would be great," Bud replied as he rubbed the side of his head and tried to sort out the sudden change of events.

"I'll be right back; it's in my lunchbox." He walked back up to the apartment with Badger on his heels. He went into the living room and opened his lunchbox that still sat on the coffee table. The key had settled to the bottom. He seldom used it, as there always seemed to be someone around the group toolbox. He dug around and then pulled the key out and started to walk out the door but stopped instantly in his tracks. He slowly turned to face his right and then stared at the double doors. His eyes squinted at the doors in disbelief. Both stood wide open just as they had been the previous morning.

Bud stood firm in the living room, examining them to believe what he was seeing. In his mind, he quickly retraced the events of the night before. The doors were closed and locked; he knew that because he tried to go through them to get his club after he'd heard the scream. He walked between the doors, scanning up and down both. They were wide open, just as they had been until the previous night. He then closed them from inside the bedroom.

Bud looked around the antique-style door handles for the lock. There wasn't a lock on these doors. He looked all around the frame for perhaps an unusual lock that may be difficult to see. After a thorough search, he concluded that the doors had never held a lock on them, to begin with.

Opening the doors wide again, he walked outside to Donnie's pickup. As he came closer, he noticed Donnie gazing up at a second-floor window of the apartments. It was the same one Bud had discovered the night before as being burned out. He turned his attention up to the room also, thinking maybe Donnie had noticed somehow the apartment was burned out. But he could see nothing that would indicate from the outside that it had burned on the inside.

As he came closer to the pickup, Donnie immediately asked, "Hey, what's the girl's name in that apartment up there?"

Bud again looked back up at the apartment Donnie had pointed to in a sense of disbelief that his friend could be asking such a question. Then, he turned back to Donnie, thinking surely, he must be playing a joke on him. His friend had a sincere face and no sign of anything else. If he was playing a joke on Bud, he must be a master of acting.

Bud considered the situation for a few seconds. He almost blurted out the burned condition of the room. But before he spoke, a thought came to him. It was an exciting idea, and he took a breath to refocus his thoughts. He calmed down and expressed no emotion toward Donnie. If Donnie really did see a girl in that window, he would be able to describe her.

"I'm not really sure which girl you're talking about. What did she look like?"

Donnie didn't hesitate. "She looked about your age, maybe early twenties; she had long brown hair and a hair tie that pulled it back."

"Did you see what she was wearing?"

"She was wearing a beige dress that was shiny, maybe silk or something. It looked a little out of date, but I don't know much about fashion. She had a hair tie that matched the dress, I think."

The young man was amazed at the description and tried to quickly think of anything else to get more information from Donnie.

"So, what did she do? Did she say something to you?"

Donnie stared at Bud, seeming puzzled by the continuing questions.

"No, she didn't say anything." He paused as if recalling the event, "She stood in the window looking out. I waved at her. I think she saw me, but she didn't wave back. She just went back into the apartment. I was hoping she would come down here."

Struggling to find another query for information, Bud asked, "Was there anyone else with her?"

By this time, Donnie knew something was up.

"Do you know her name or not? That's all I'm asking you." He continued before Bud could say anything and obviously felt somewhat perturbed at being strung along, "If you don't know her, that's fine. If you have a line on her, that's fine as well. I'm not trying to horn in on you, Buddy. I just thought since you're going to Reston and I'm staying here the rest of the week, and if she's single, maybe you could introduce me to her. I could give you the week's rent you paid; you know, I could stay here the rest of the week, maybe ask her out."

Bud glanced at Donnie and then back up at the apartment window, trying desperately to find an intelligent and acceptable reply. He had led Donnie on to get answers, and now Donnie was the one who wanted answers. Donnie shrugged his shoulder a little and raised his hand to indicate he was expecting a reply. Bud realized now the only acceptable answer would be the truth, and then, if Donnie didn't accept it, he would still have done the right thing.

He took a deep breath and said what he had to say.

"There's no one else living in these apartments but me, Donnie. All the other apartments are locked uptight, and I'm absolutely sure of that." He paused. "In fact, the apartment up there where you saw the girl, it's completely burned out on the inside; you can't see it from out here because of the screens."

Donnie stared at him the way someone might look at a car salesman after discovering he'd been trying to scam him into buying a lemon.

"Why are you trying to give me the runaround, Bud? If you don't know the girl, just say so."

He now stared at Donnie without any emotion. He wanted to say something but couldn't think of anything else to tell his friend.

After a few seconds, a strange expression came over Donnie's face, maybe the way someone would look after getting too close to a snake. He slowly moved back into his pickup, resting his right arm on the steering wheel.

"You're serious, aren't you?"

"Yeah. I know it sounds strange, Donnie, but it's the truth."

"Strange?" Donnie now seemed to be having trouble taking all of it in.

"You mean to tell me, you've been living in that house, all this time, with a ghost?"

Bud turned back, he glanced at the large house for a second and then turned his attention back to Donnie.

"Actually, I'm almost certain there's more than one."

Donnie reached over and started his pickup after Bud said this.

"You are crazy, Bud." He put his pickup into gear. "No, you are plumb out of your skull, Buddy."

Bud just nodded a little. Then, remembering the key to the group toolbox was still in his hand. He held it up.

"Oh, here's the key."

Donnie took the key and tossed it in the ashtray, then leaned down, peering back up at the window briefly, then glanced back at Bud.

"That's just too weird, man, way too weird." He then quickly drove away.

Chapter Five:

A SAD TALE

After Donnie left, Bud turned around and faced the looming old mansion. He suddenly felt very alone. Reaching down to Badger, who sat beside him, he patted his dog on the head. He then walked back into the apartment and prepared some breakfast.

The day moved close to noon before he began loading up the Pontiac with his few belongings. He put Badger on the run line to keep him out of the way.

After placing some items in the trunk, he turned to go back into the house. He then noticed the elderly woman next door walking out on her porch and sitting down with a cup in her hand.

Bud watched her for a moment, trying to decide if he should go talk to her or not. The last time he tried, she acted a little startled by him approaching her. After considering that this would likely be his last chance to get answers about the old house, he shut the trunk lid and walked over to her house.

As he stepped up to the porch, the woman sat staring off into the sky toward her right, seeming to gaze out over the treetops. He wondered if she may be watching some birds or something. Bud stood at the bottom of her porch for a few seconds hoping she would notice him. Then, after she didn't, he cleared his throat to get her attention.

"Oh," the woman said, as she was obviously a bit surprised and almost spilled her drink.

"I'm sorry, madam; I didn't mean to startle you."

The woman briefly placed her hand on her chest, but then calmed down and sat back.

"Well, that's all right, young man; I'm simply too easy to startle nowadays. Can I help you?"

"I hope so, madam. I've been living in the apartments next door, and I wondered if you could tell me anything about the original house."

The woman stared at Bud for a second. Then, she took a drink from her cup, holding it with both hands and seemingly using the pause to consider what she wanted to do before speaking. After her drink, she slowly put her cup on the wicker table that matched the other furniture on the porch.

"Would you like to join me in a cup of tea, young man?"

He didn't need to think twice about his answer.

"Yes, I would love that."

The woman stood up and went into the house. Bud walked up the steps of the front porch and sat down in the wicker chair opposite to where the elderly lady sat. Soon, she came back out carrying what appeared to be an antique Asian tea set on a platter. She sat down and began pouring a cup of tea for Bud.

"Would you like some sugar or cream in your tea?"

"I'll take sugar, please."

The woman put a spoon of sugar in the cup, stirred it around and handed it to Bud.

"No one seems to drink hot tea anymore. It's a shame I'd say." She poured some more tea in her cup.

"Mamie Hunt," she said, picking her cup up and then glancing at Bud.

"Excuse me?"

"My name, it's Mamie Hunt."

"Oh, I'm sorry, Bud Fisher," reaching over the table, Bud offered his hand to shake.

Mamie set her tea down, smiled slightly and gently shook his hand. Bud suddenly realized this may not be the most appropriate gesture for this elegant elderly lady, and feeling a bit embarrassed about the realization, put his hand back down rather awkwardly.

She then picked her cup up again and examined Bud across the rim as she took another sip. She slowly lowered the cup, holding it with both hands in her lap.

"I've seen you and your dog outside from time to time, Mr. Bud Fisher. So, tell me, what exactly is your interest in the old Cooper place?"

Bud picked up his cup. He wasn't a big tea drinker, but he took his time with the cup as he considered a place to start.

After a sip, he sat the cup down and began as best he could.

"Well, there's a room upstairs that's been burned out. Is there anything you can tell me about that?"

Mamie again stared at Bud, as if trying to decide what she wanted to say. Then, in a matter of fact manner, she slowly began.

"There was a young girl, about your age, I believe. She died in a fire. It was in that very room a long time ago, before I was born, in fact. Since the accident, the room has been rebuilt and burned out again, at least three times that I'm aware of."

He stared at the elderly woman in amazement from what she had just told him. He casually picked his teacup back up, never losing sight of Mamie. She then raised her cup to take a drink. Just before taking a drink, though, she gazed down at the tea inside her cup, as she held it close to her mouth, and then said something, almost in a whisper.

"I've often seen her, standing in the window, gazing out." Mamie then slowly took a drink of her tea.

Bud sat frozen with his teacup halfway up to the position of taking a drink. Never once turning to look at him, she lowered the cup and continued in the same soft voice.

"My children believe I'm crazy."

She put her cup on the table and gazed down at her lap. She pressed the palms of her hands along her dress and around her knees, ironing out some unseen imperfection. Bud watched her closely, completely fixated on this woman that he now knew had answers for his questions.

After smoothing out the tiny wrinkles or perhaps removing moisture from her hands, Mamie finally turned back to Bud. She had a keen expression of inquiry on her face. Bud, still sitting frozen with the teacup in a ready position, realized she expected him to speak now.

She'd told him something that she wouldn't tell just anyone. He now reasoned that she also wanted some clarity from him, someone with no actual connections to her. She wanted answers from a person who had stayed in the house, the same house that had put her family into a position of questioning her sanity.

It seemed to him, they sat staring at each other for several minutes, though it was likely only a few seconds. Mamie never backed down; she gazed straight into the young man's eyes, waiting for his reply. She'd given him time to think and now expected a remark from him. Bud struggled for something to say. Finally, he blurted out the only thing he knew to be a truthful statement.

"You're not crazy, Mamie."

She smiled, though not a smile of happiness. This appeared to be more a smile of vindication. She then carefully poured a little more tea in her cup, added a small amount of sugar and stirred it.

At this point, Bud took the drink that had been frozen for some time and returned the cup to the table. Mamie began to speak again, and as she did, Bud could imagine the scenes in his mind, almost as if reading a novel or newspaper.

"The Cooper house is the oldest one in this area. The house is certainly over a hundred years old by now; I'm not certain how old it is, though. I was about fourteen at the time I moved here with my family." She paused and gazed out over the trees as if recalling those long-gone days of her youth. Then, she glanced at Bud and back to her teacup. With another quick breath, she went on.

"Six years later, I got married and moved from Madison. My husband and I raised our children in St. Louis, Missouri. Years went by, and my father passed away. Shortly afterward, my husband passed away, as well. My mother was living in this big house alone, so I came to stay with her. She eventually passed on, and here I am now.

"No one seems to know the stories of the old Cooper house these days, and no one seems to care much. Most of the stories dealing with the history of the Cooper house are the ones I heard as a teenage girl; if they're true or not, I can't say.

"The old folks around Madison said James Cooper married for money. He'd inherited some money but squandered most of it away. Martha, however, was born into a wealthy family.

"No one knew who Jenny's real father was. From what people put together afterward, Jenny seems to have been a love child, born out of wedlock. Martha's family sent her to Europe to have the child and meanwhile circulated a story of Martha marrying in Europe and the father dying of some sudden illness.

"The situation had become a problem for Martha's family, as people talked and asked questions. When James Cooper came along, he likely seemed to be a convenient solution. By way of marriage, the prominent family could get Martha and Jenny away and avoid additional controversy. Somehow, whether by her family making the decision or maybe the deal had been made with James, the exact reason is unknown. Yet, somehow the three ended up in Madison with a lot of money.

"The house was built sometime before the turn of the century. I heard a date of 1877, but I don't know if that's an accurate date or not. At the time, what quickly became known as the 'Cooper house' was the only one around this area of Madison. More came soon after, though, as those who craved prestige thought the prime place must surely be close to the magnificent house.

"James dabbled in business around town, but mostly he seemed to act as if he were a big shot. As time went by, Jenny grew into a beautiful young lady. The young men began to take an interest in Jenny, but her stepfather wouldn't let her have anything to do with any of them. Again, and again, she wasn't allowed to see any of the young suitors who wanted to court her.

"There were suspicions about the true nature of her stepfather's motives. James would say there wasn't a young man around who was good enough for his stepdaughter. Her mother tried to talk him into letting her go to college. This, however, was at a time when women in this area seldom went to college, and James refused. Regardless of why he wouldn't let her far from his clutches, Jenny became understandingly despondent about the situation.

"Even with her stepfather's overprotective nature, she somehow met a young man, and the two fell in love. Through the tight security that surrounded Jenny, the two of them managed to make plans to run away and elope without her stepfather's consent. She was twenty years old, and it has been said, she planned to leave the night before she turned twenty-one, which was the legal age of an adult at that time. Either way, they had a plan to get away from her stepfather.

"How James found out about the plan no one really knows. Also, there seems to be a conflict of information about whether he threatened the young man and frightened him away without Jenny knowing, or if the accident occurred before he was set to arrive and take Jenny away.

"Jenny dressed and got herself ready that afternoon. She didn't know her stepfather had become aware of their plans, and she watched out the window anxiously. James Cooper, meanwhile, sat downstairs, indignantly drinking and becoming quite intoxicated.

"Finally, after the sun went down, Jenny lit her oil lamp, still peering out the window, looking for the young man to arrive and take her from an overbearing stepfather. James Cooper, having become completely inebriated by now, staggered up the stairs. He went into Jenny's room, and they soon became engaged in an intense argument. Her mother, being afraid of her alcoholic husband, remained downstairs, too frightened to do anything on her daughter's behalf.

"After arguing fiercely about the young man, it is thought that James may have slapped Jenny, and she fell onto the bed in tears. Others said she simply fell onto the bed, crying. James then backed into or bumped against the table, holding the lamp as he left the room. The lamp fell onto a folded quilt beside the table, making little noise."

James slammed the door shut, took his key and locked it. He then stormed down the stairs. He set his key on a table and returned to his chair and drank more.

"By the time Jenny realized the lamp had fallen, the fire had become large. She tried to get out, but the door was locked. She screamed, but James initially thought she was just mad. However, her mother knew something had to be wrong and yelled at James to act."

"James went up the stairs and became shocked seeing fire from under the door. He reached into his pocket for the key, but it wasn't there. He ran down the stairs and retrieved the key from the table. Back up the stairs, he went. He opened the door; by this time, the fire was raging.

"He somehow got a sheet or a cover of some sort and doused it with water. He fought the fire furiously. Help arrived from somewhere. Some say a neighbor saw the smoke. Others say that Jenny's mother went outside and screamed for help.

"James was severely injured by the flames, but he managed to somehow save the house from burning down. He couldn't save Jenny, though. James Cooper couldn't be moved from the house, and after several days of agony, he died from his injuries. Before he died, he bemoaned the incident and it being an accident, as he went in and out of consciousness."

Mamie stopped here and gazed out over the treetops as she'd been doing when Bud unintentionally startled her.

Bud had lost all track of time while listening to this elegant lady. He picked up his tea and took a drink. The tea had become cold, but he didn't mind. When he sat it back down on the table, Mamie picked up the Asian teapot and poured his cup full and then filled hers as well.

She then picked up her cup and took a drink, then sat her hands down in her lap with the teacup clasped in them. She again moved her attention over the treetops, as if meditating on a favorite poem or remembering a special Christmas with her family. Bud thought this must be a favorite spot for Mamie to look out to and relax.

He again picked his teacup up and took another drink. It seemed she had answered many of the questions about the house. Then, he thought of the window, and this, in turn, brought the double doors to mind.

"Do you know anything about a window downstairs that won't stay closed, or a set of double doors that close and lock when there's no lock on them?"

Mamie turned to Bud, seeming a little surprised, as a mother might look at a child who had just asked for more asparagus or green peas. She peered down at the cup in her hands, then ran a finger around part of the rim. For a few seconds, Bud thought she might know nothing about these things. Then, his patience was rewarded as Mamie began again.

"Martha Cooper was, of course, devastated by the accident and consequently had some form of breakdown not long after. Once it was repaired, she closed off the upstairs. When someone visited her, she always had a window open regardless of it being winter or summer.

"From what people pieced together, she claimed not being able to get the burned smell out of the house. Most people thought it wasn't the smell of the burned room she spoke of, but rather James and Jenny.

"The doctors prescribed medications for her, most likely narcotics. As time went by, she became dependent and used the medications more and more. Often, she wouldn't be seen outside the house for months at a time, having her food and other items delivered by errand boys. Eventually, she stayed mainly in one room, downstairs, and in the front part of the house.

"Incidentally, it was one of the errand boys who alerted people of Martha's passing. He was making a regular delivery when Martha didn't come to the door. Finding this unusual, he opened the door slightly and spotted her dead on the floor. The doctors determined that she'd used too much medication and died of an overdose.

"The house stood empty for some time but eventually went into cycles of being bought and resold over the years; as generally happens to many older houses. Time after time, people would move in, only to move back out not long after.

"In the nineteen twenties, it became what was politely called an upscale cat house. During this time, the room upstairs burned again, quite mysteriously. Only the one room burned, and from what was reported, it burned and then seemed to strangely extinguish itself before causing any more damage. Once again, the house went empty.

"When my family and I moved here, the house stood vacant and rather spooky to me. Then, someone from out of town, possibly thinking they had stumbled onto a steal, bought it and repaired the room. As had become routine by now, they moved in and then moved out shortly afterward. Once again, the house went up for sale. For the six years I lived here during my teens, the house remained empty for the most part.

"I suspect my mother had either seen something or sensed something because she would tell me time after time to stay away from the house. I needed little coaxing from her to avoid the vacant old home.

"I didn't think much about the stories of the Coopers after the initial excitement of hearing them. My friends would sometimes comment on the house being haunted, but I think the town's business folk played these stories down as much as possible. They realized the house would sell to some investor from out of town and, in the process, bring money into Madison.

"After I moved away, I seldom thought of the old place. When I visited on occasion, I would hear a few tales and find it would be standing empty more often than not. During the fifties, Jenny's room burned again; this time, the circumstances proved even stranger, as no one lived in the house. The room and fire, as before, burned itself out.

"Then, ten or twelve years later, an outside investor bought the house with the great idea of making apartments. The work crews came in and renovated it, repairing the burned room and turning the once-grand home into common apartments.

"Initially, quite an interest stirred around the apartments. They filled rather quickly, as this area was still considered something of a nice neighborhood, even if somewhat aged. Slowly, however, one by one, they began moving out until the apartments stood empty once again.

"John Beldon came to town and bought the apartments not long after moving here. He must have thought like so many others before him, that he was getting a great bargain. He bought several other rental properties, and they always stayed rented out. The apartments, however, remained empty. Then, maybe five or six years ago, the apartment burned out again. Mr. Beldon sent a repair crew to work on it, but before they accomplished much, he called them off. It seemed he'd finally heard the stories and decided against putting any more money into the old house. This brings the tale to the present, the two of us sitting on a porch, talking about strange things we don't really understand."

Mamie smiled at Bud and then shifted her gaze back to the spot out over the trees that she seemed so fond of.

Bud felt as if he'd just finished running a foot race. He felt tired yet satisfied in the knowledge he now had of the old house. He poured some more tea for himself and took a drink. He then held his cup in his lap and gazed out to the spot where Mamie remained transfixed.

He sat with her for a while longer, enjoying the day and considering the story she'd told him. He told her before leaving that she'd explained a lot and reassured her not to worry about her mental state.

Bud finished packing his belongings. He took down the run line and made one final walk through the apartment. He now saw the rooms in a completely different way.

He thought to himself, *this is a sad old house with sad and lonely memories.* As he prepared to leave, he noticed the window and realized he had one more thing to do. Retrieving the hammer from his car, he pulled the nail from the window frame. He then opened it back up to the mark he'd made on the framework. Bud then walked out to the car, where Badger waited in the passenger seat.

"All right, boy, I guess we're ready."

He put the car in reverse and backed out of the drive, then pulled forward to where his driver's window faced the house. He wanted to take one last look. He stared at the big elegant house, trying to take a mental picture.

Suddenly, he noticed movement in the burned-out room. Jenny walked up to the window and gazed out. She was young and beautiful, just as Donnie had described her.

A sensation of fear ran up Bud's back, but he refused to turn away. He stared straight at her, trying to memorize something he knew to be rare, and few people would ever get a chance to see. She looked out as if waiting for someone. After a moment, she moved away from the window.

Bud took a slow deep breath as if he'd just walked from a smoky room. He then turned to Badger, saddened by the sight he'd just beheld.

"She's still waiting for him."

Badger turned to his master with an expression of having no concern in the world. The sight of his carefree dog caused him to chuckle a little. He reached up and pushed his dog's head softly in a loving gesture. He then put the Pontiac in drive, and they rolled away. He would never see the house on Cooper Lane again.

The End

We hope you enjoyed The House on Cooper Lane. As an added bonus we've included Oliver Phipps' best-selling short story, Twelve Minute Till Midnight. We hope you enjoy it.

TWELVE MINUTES TILL MIDNIGHT

Gray Door Ltd.

The Days of Reckoning

A swarm of cicadas filled the warm day of May 1934 with their chorus of screeching songs. Suddenly, the insects halted their long chirps and an eerie silence overtook the dusty Louisiana road.

After a moment of the unnatural quiet, a man of around forty, in well-worn clothes and holding a ragged coat in his arm, stood up from beside the road.

He was common in appearance yet stood tall and held an air of dignity about himself, even in his weathered apparel.

He moved slowly to the road's edge and stood watching down the long stretch of gravel.

Soon, a dark colored Ford sedan came traveling toward him at a rapid pace. The car came into view with a contrail of dust billowing behind.

As soon as the sedan passed by the man, brakes were applied, causing the car to slide a bit and come to a noisy halt about twenty yards past him.

The man beside the road turned, and as if anticipating the arrival of a car, began walking through the dust toward it.

As he came closer, a sweaty young man got out of the front passenger door and walked to the back of the car. He opened the rear driver's side door and looked back down the road to where the man now stood.

"I'm riding back here." The young man said in a rough voice and then climbed into the back seat.

The man walked around to the passenger side of the car and seeing a woman laying in the back seat, he opened the front passenger door.

The driver also appeared rough and had sweat beads on his forehead.

A musk smell mixed with cigarettes and whiskey resonated inside the interior of the automobile.

Once the doors shut, the young man in the back said, "Let's go Henry," and the driver took off quickly, causing the tires to spin rocks and dust into the air behind them.

Warm air entered the car through the open windows and allowed a small amount of reprieve from the humid Louisiana heat.

Henry was a young man in his early twenties. He appeared nervous as he drove the Ford sedan, glancing toward the man with suspicion in his eyes.

The passenger now noticed that Henry had a pistol sitting between his legs. The edgy young driver looked over toward him again and then glanced at the rearview mirror on the passenger door.

He began to speak in a low, aggressive voice. "Don't be getting any ideas." He again glanced at both side mirrors, as if someone might come up quickly behind them. Then he checked the rearview mirror and continued in the same tone.

"You know that's Bonnie and Clyde back there don't you?"

The passenger glanced back at the two people in the back. They appeared tired and uncomfortable. They seemed to be sleeping or trying to sleep. The passenger turned back to the driver.

"I was just catching a ride. Maybe I should be getting out now." He said politely with a southern drawl.

Henry smirked at this. He again checked the mirrors as the car juggled around from the rough gravel roads. "There ain't anyone getting out now, unless Clyde says so. Or we all die in a hail of bullets."

The passenger again glanced at the pistol between the driver's legs before he turned to the front windshield.

Suddenly a large bug connected violently against the windshield directly in front of him, causing him to flinch. Henry chuckled a little at this. The passenger turned to Henry and watched him a few seconds. He then turned his attention to the scenery passing by outside his window.

After almost an hour of driving, they pulled down a side road. There stood the remnants of a house. From what could be seen, a fire likely destroyed the home and after years of abandonment only fragments of the original structure could be seen.

Henry and the passenger climbed out and began to stretch a little. Clyde exited the rear door of the car and quickly limped around to the other door. He opened this one and carefully assisted Bonnie out. She appeared to have a wounded leg. She limped with Clyde's help to a stump and laid against it.

Clyde pulled two cigarettes from a pack in his pocket. He quickly lit both and handed Bonnie one. She immediately began to pull drags from the cigarette, as if desperate for the nicotine, and then blew the smoke out quickly so she could pull another drag from it. The grayish blue smoke briefly floated around her before disappearing.

After watching this, the older man that was picked up from the roadside found some brick remains of a porch support and sat down facing the two, while Henry scanned the area in a manner to detect any unseen threats.

Clyde retrieved a few things from the back seat of the car and then the trunk. He tucked a pistol under his belt, and placed several bottles of whiskey on a flat area close to Bonnie.

"Go see if you can get some gas, and cigarettes; maybe something to eat too." Clyde sounded winded as he told Henry this.

Henry nodded and left quickly in the car.

Clyde placed a folded jacket behind Bonnie and gave her a drink from a whiskey bottle. She coughed a little after taking a drink. When she coughed, she grimaced in pain and held her leg. She lay back on the stump and closed her eyes.

The afternoon waned. Clyde began to move about, gathering pieces of wood and placing them into a pile. The man watched Clyde with apprehension but said nothing. The outlaw in turn continued to glance over at the man from time to time.

The man was older than Clyde. He could see Clyde must be in his early to mid-twenties. Yet the young man appeared tired and spent. After several tense moments of watching each other the older man spoke.

"I don't believe I belong here. I'll be moving along."

Clyde sneered at the man. "You may not belong here, but you're here now. You got a problem with the company you keep?"

The older man said nothing but picked up a stick and raked it on the ground in a drawing fashion.

Clyde continued. "You don't look so important to me. What good are you? All the good folks out there that don't want anything to do with Bonnie and me; they all got some occupation they pride themselves highly of. So what is it you're good for?"

The man casually dropped the stick and gazed at the ground when Clyde asked him this. He then folded his ragged coat and repositioned it over his leg in a manner suggesting he wouldn't be leaving soon. After a few seconds he replied to Clyde, but without much zeal.

"I've done some writing over the years. But folks haven't been reading my work much lately. Now days I just seem to wander around here and there; sort of like the wind I suppose, speaking, where folks will have me; in churches and community buildings sometimes. But most folks seem to want someone to talk to rather than do any listening."

Clyde chuckled at this as he knelt down to light some scraps of paper under the small pile of wood.

"Yeah, times are tough all over ain't they? You sound like a preacher to me. That's what all those high and mighty preachers like to do, write stuff and then talk to people. Tell folks how bad they are and how they're all going to hell. Are you a preacher?"

The fire began to slowly blaze as Clyde asked the man this.

"No." The man said, almost in a whisper.

"Yeah, well, I think you're the same thing as a preacher whether you admit it or not."

Clyde blew lightly on the small fire after saying this. The fire became a little larger as he did.

Once the fire took hold and began to burn on its own Clyde stood back up. He walked over to Bonnie and checked on her. She lay asleep, though rustling about occasionally as if uncomfortable.

He then sat back down; staring at the small fire and glancing up at the man from time to time. The evening stressed toward night as the two men eyed each other.

Clyde flipped his cigarette into the fire and stood up. He moved over to the whiskey bottles and picked one up. He took a drink and wiped his mouth on his shirt sleeve. He pulled another cigarette out of the pack with his mouth as he stared across the fire at the man.

Once his cigarette had been lit and he'd taken a long drag from it, he spoke again as he exhaled the smoke and paced slowly around the fire.

"I've been wanting to tell someone the real truth of things. You look like someone that'll know the truth when you see it."

The young outlaw took another long drag and expelled it toward the sky. He thought for a second and then continued.

"You see Preacher, Bonnie and me; we're doing all the good people a favor, even though they don't seem to realize it. We're fighting all the corrupt government people and the bankers that take people's land. We should be heroes. The truth of the matter is the government trains people to go out and kill. And they say it's all right when soldiers do that for the government. But they call Bonnie and me 'murderers.'"

Clyde took another drag from the cigarette as Preacher watched from the other side of the fire. He spewed the smoke out quickly and continued. "And the government takes people's land. They steal good folk's land from them. They kick them off their own land and call that repossession for past due taxes. But they call Bonnie and me 'robbers.' So, you see Preacher, we're the good ones, cause we're fighting for all those folks out there that won't fight. That is the truth Preacher, that is the real truth."

Clyde took another drink of whiskey as if to stress his statement before he looked over at Preacher with interest.

Preacher sat silent. He gazed down at his feet and rubbed the worn toe of his shoe in the dirt. Clyde took another long drag from his cigarette and blew the smoke out as he gazed off into the evening sky.

Finally, Preacher looked up at Clyde and in a stern voice asked.

"Is that the truth Clyde? Is that the real truth?"

Clyde froze in place when Preacher asked him this. He turned and stared at Preacher with a slight anger in his eyes. He took another drag from his cigarette and appeared to consider Preacher's question briefly before replying.

"Everybody thinks they know all about the truth. Everyone has their opinion about the truth. But all those opinions are different. The truth is, Bonnie and me are just defending ourselves. I want everyone to know that. That's my truth Preacher. We're just defending ourselves from the law. We're just trying to survive. We're not bad. The law is the one that's bad. If the law would leave us alone there wouldn't be any reason to fight."

He then stared at Preacher in anticipation of an answer. He quickly lifted the bottle up for another drink. He wiped his mouth on his sleeve again then the sweat from his forehead.

Preacher used his forearms to lean on his legs. He gazed down at the ground between them as if searching for some hidden object. Darkness now took over and the fire began to create splashes of light around them.

As seconds passed by and the embers from the small fire danced high into the air, Clyde again glanced at Preacher. He smiled due to the long pause.

But then Preacher took a deep breath and replied with clear and unfaltering words. "You may speak what you consider to be the truth for you and Bonnie. But generally speaking, you're still wrong. And the general nature of that wrong defeats any truth you may hold on your own."

Now Clyde became animated and reacted to Preacher in anger.

"What is that? You tell me Preacher, why you think, what you just said, has anything to do with anything. No one can say what the truth is or isn't. If you know what the truth is then you tell me Preacher. You tell me right now what the truth of anything is."

Preacher never looked up as Clyde said this. Instead he continued to scan the ground between his legs. But after Clyde finished making his statement Preacher casually looked up at him and replied calmly.

"I believe the truth is, every man knows right from wrong deep down inside. And this is a universal truth. Not the truth a person builds up around them by their own deeds. And every man and woman must face this truth in some form or fashion before they die."

Clyde stared at Preacher. He seemed surprised that he actually had an answer. Preacher in turn continued with his assessment after a brief pause.

"Whether people accept this, shall we say, 'spirit of truth' or not, doesn't change it Clyde. Whether a man allows himself to see truth or not won't eliminate its existence. But everyone will face the truth in some way. Each man and woman will have the opportunity to do the right thing. And this fact is one of those 'real truths' that no man will ever be able to alter by his own devices or actions."

Clyde continued to stare at Preacher with contempt. Then he turned to Bonnie. She was sitting up, staring into the fire. Clyde looked back at Preacher and sort of nodded at Bonnie, as if he'd woken her.

"How long have you been up Sugar?"

Bonnie moved a little and grimaced in pain as she did so. "Long enough," she replied flatly. "Give me a cigarette, would you?"

Clyde pulled a pack of cigarettes out and lit one. He handed it to Bonnie. Then he sat down beside her and pulled a cigarette out for himself.

Bonnie stared across the fire at Preacher. She pulled a drag from her cigarette and exhaled the smoke quickly.

Clyde handed her the whiskey bottle. She took a drink and her face twisted as she swallowed. Just as she put the cigarette into her mouth again a car could be heard turning down the lonely road.

Clyde stood and pulled the pistol from his belt. He stared with apprehension at the head lights rolling slowly toward them.

"It is Henry." He tucked the pistol back into his belt. Bonnie laid back as she could also see the familiar sedan moving closer.

Henry hopped out of the car, turning the headlights out as he did so.

"Anyone recognize you?" Clyde asked as Henry opened the back door of the car.

"I don't think so. I went to a small store on the edge of town that had just one old man working. He seemed too tired to care about anything."

Preacher noticed that Henry seemed to fear Clyde as much as respecting him. He was also obviously a little younger than Clyde. Preacher sat quietly and watched the unusual relationship with interest. Clyde treated Henry as an employee, but then also seemed to treat him as a grunt at times.

Henry pulled a sack from the back seat. He then pulled various food items and cigarettes out of the bag, setting them down with the items Clyde had beside the fire. As he stood back up Henry glanced over at Preacher. He said nothing to him and Preacher watched Henry with apprehension.

As Clyde and Bonnie began to eat, Henry went back to the car and retrieved another sack. This sack had several large bottles of whiskey and another bottle that Preacher couldn't tell for sure what the contents were.

They sat around the fire eating while Preacher watched. Then Clyde threw part of a loaf of bread over to Preacher.

After examining the loaf on the ground a few seconds, he reached down and gingerly picked it up. He then closed his eyes briefly. After a couple seconds he opened them up and began to eat the bread in small bites. As he did this, he glanced over to Clyde who now chuckled under his breath and sneered slightly at Preacher.

Later Clyde, Bonnie and Henry sat around the fire. They smoked cigarettes one after the other. They drank and played cards without stopping. Around midnight Preacher pulled his coat over himself and lay on the ground watching them until finally falling asleep.

The next morning, crackling embers of the dying fire greeted Preacher as he opened his eyes. Dampness persisted in the air. He sat up. The sun had not broken across the horizon yet. There sat Clyde across the smoldering fire, staring at Preacher with hollow, emotionless eyes.

Preacher looked at Bonnie and Henry as they lay asleep with thin blankets tossed over them. As he sat up, Preacher quickly turned his eyes back to Clyde and now refused to turn away or show weakness. Clyde in turn continued to sit stoically; examining Preacher in silence. The two remained in this state for several moments as the others slept.

When the light of the sun broke, causing a few rays to stream across Preachers face, Clyde began to speak in a low voice. He struggled to sound friendly and more civilized than the previous night.

"All the good folks are saying Bonnie and I are killers and bad people. They should know we're just trying to defend ourselves from corrupt law people. Bonnie and I are fighting for all those good folks out there because they don't have the gumption to fight for themselves."

Clyde took a quick drag from his cigarette and continued as the smoke came from his mouth. "Someone like you could tell them our side of it and they would listen to you. If you told the people we're out here fighting their fight, they might listen."

Preacher watched Clyde closely as he said this. Then he replied to Clyde after very little thought.

"I can't tell the people such a thing."

Clyde appeared puzzled by this answer. His voice became more hostile.

"You're supposed to be so good. You said yourself that you do speaking and writing. You said yourself you've attended churches. What do you mean you won't tell the people?"

Preacher picked up a small stone and tossed it into the remnants of the fire, causing tiny glowing embers to fly upwards. Then he replied as he watched the smoldering campfire.

"A man has a right to defend himself from an aggressor just as a country or even a town has the right to defend itself. It does this by asking a few of the citizens to fight the threat for the good of all the people. Are you defending yourself Clyde, or are you the aggressor?"

Preacher paused for a second as if in thought, and then continued.

"Unless the people asked you to fight for them, you ain't fighting for the people. You're fighting for yourself. Did any of those good folks you speak of ask you to do what you're doing?"

Clyde's mouth twisted with anger when Preacher said this. He took another drag from his cigarette and spewed the smoke out.

Just as Clyde was about to also spew a mouth full of curses out, Preacher turned to look at Bonnie. Clyde then also turned and looked at Bonnie. He realized she lay awake, gazing out across the dying fire.

"Give me a cigarette Clyde." She said with a weary voice.

Clyde pulled a cigarette from the pack and lit it for Bonnie. He handed the cigarette to her and she quickly began to pull a drag from it with urgency. He returned to his makeshift sitting spot and stared at Preacher with anger.

Preacher in turn watched Clyde with a quiet resolve. Occasionally he raked a small stick on the ground between his legs but otherwise didn't express weakness to the outlaw.

Soon Henry stirred and after a few bites of leftover food they all began to load into the car. Clyde assisted Bonnie into the back seat and with a flash of Clyde's pistol Preacher once again moved reluctantly to the front passenger seat.

As the car rumbled down the rough back roads Henry turned toward the passenger seat from time to time. Preacher glanced back at Henry but neither said anything. Bonnie smoked one cigarette after another.

Clyde continued to nurse a bottle of whiskey. He still seemed angry and when Preacher turned to look at him, he still had wrath in his eyes. Eventually Preacher simply watched the scenery go by.

Later in the afternoon they came close to a town. Clyde had Henry pull into a gas station and an attendant filled the car with gas.

Henry went inside and bought several more packs of cigarettes along with some sandwiches.

Preacher noticed Bonnie and Clyde sat in the back attempting to appear normal. They acted as if they were talking together in an effort to avoid revealing their faces to the attendant.

As the attendant washed the windshield he briefly stared straight at Preacher. And then he glanced back at Bonnie and Clyde as the two continued their charade of chatting together.

After the attendant finished with the windshield he moved around to the back of the car and this caused Bonnie and Clyde to relax some.

Preacher again glanced back at Clyde who checked out the back as the attendant continued his work. Clyde turned and looked at Preacher; then pulled his coat away from his waist to reveal his pistol. Preacher turned back to the front of the car and stared out.

After returning to the car, Henry started the sedan up and they drove quietly through the back streets of town. Once on the other side, the car picked up speed and soon they were far away. The Louisiana backwoods swallowed them up as Henry ventured onto familiar roads.

Then he turned down a narrow, seldom traveled road. The grass grew in the middle of this road and only the two-wheel tracks could be seen. Under the car the grass brushed the floorboards.

After traveling the primitive road about a half mile, Henry pulled off to the side of a creek and placed the car in a semi-hidden spot behind some small trees and brush. Then everyone wearily climbed out of the car.

A barren area, of around thirty feet, lay beside the creek. It was where the creek had risen and receded causing only rock and small stones to abide now.

"We'll stay here for a little while just in case anyone in town noticed us. Later we can get back on the road. We should still make it back to your Pa's place before dark."

After saying this Clyde helped Bonnie sit beside the car and immediately, she lit up a cigarette. Henry nodded in agreement and brought the sandwiches out. Then he pulled several large pieces of logs closer to sit on.

Preacher sat and watched them eat. Again, Clyde watched him closely as if waiting for him to ask for some food. Preacher said nothing, however. When they'd almost finished eating, Clyde reached into the paper bag and pulled out half a sandwich. He sat it on the log and then glanced over to Preacher. He lit up a cigarette as Henry and Bonnie finished their meal. He smoked his cigarette slowly and continued to watch Preacher.

When Henry finished his meal, he stood and stretched. "I'm going to go keep watch." He then walked off toward the obscure road.

Clyde nodded. Seeing Bonnie had finished her sandwich he lit another cigarette and handed it to her. She climbed into the back seat of the car and sort of laid back in the seat as she smoked her cigarette.

When everything became quiet, Clyde took the half sandwich and walked over to Preacher. He sat the food down beside him. Then, he walked back over to where he was before and sat back down.

Preacher glanced down at the sandwich. He then looked back at Clyde who again watched him closely as he lit another cigarette from the one he'd just finished.

Several minutes passed by as the two observed each other. Then Preacher reached down to pick up the sandwich. When he did this Clyde straightened a little and took hold of the pistol handle in his belt. Preacher stopped before his hand touched the food beside him.

Clyde sneered a bit and then rubbed the handle of the pistol softly. Preacher slowly moved his hand to the sandwich without showing any emotion, but also never taking his eyes from Clyde.

Picking the food up, Preacher lowered his head a few seconds and then opened his eyes and placed his gaze immediately on Clyde again. He slowly took a bite of the sandwich and chewed with caution. Clyde chuckled and then moved his hand back from the pistol.

As Preacher slowly ate, Clyde reached over and picked up a near-empty bottle of whiskey. He turned the bottle up and finished about half of the remaining liquid in one large drink. Then he wiped his mouth on his sleeve, while grimacing from the taste of the alcohol. Once he'd recovered from the drink he again stared at Preacher.

"That's just like that couple we picked up a while back; all good, upstanding and law-abiding citizens. They didn't hesitate to eat food that was bought with stolen money though. All the good people suddenly turn bad when they get hungry."

Clyde paused briefly and then continued.

"You tell me Preacher, why isn't that the truth? You're eating food bought with stolen money. You talk to me about truth and then you eat a sandwich bought with money that was stolen from a bank. Go right ahead Preacher; tell me the truth about that."

After Clyde said this, he took another long drag from his cigarette. Again, he spewed the smoke out in a rapid exhale through gritted teeth and tight lips. He stared at Preacher and then stood up. He began to pace a little in front of the log.

Preacher finished chewing a bite and gazed at the sandwich, seeming to pay little attention to Clyde.

This pause caused Clyde to become more animated. Now he laughed under his breath as he stared down at Preacher. He turned the bottle up and took another drink leaving only a small amount in the bottle.

Preacher swallowed and without looking at Clyde, began to speak.

"When a soldier is taken prisoner, he doesn't turn down the food offered to him by his enemy simply because the food was grown on enemy soil. The bread did no evil. Nor does food commit crimes. I can give a piece of this bread to a bird and it won't poison the bird. And the bird won't question the origin of the offering either.

"The wrong occurred when you forcefully took the bounty of another man's labor. The fact that your prisoners eat food derived from evil gains won't undo the initial wrong committed. And it doesn't make them guilty of your crime."

Now Clyde's face contorted in a fit of anger. Preacher watched the flush of blood flow to his face, causing his features to express an immediate and evil desire to quench the rage welling up inside him.

Clyde immediately threw the whiskey bottle at Preacher just as a loud cry of violent intent burst from his lungs, "Aaarrhhhhggggg!" Clyde's aim with the bottle was spot on. Preacher raised his arm just in time to deflect the projectile hurling toward him. The impact of the bottle caused a distinct clunking sound as it made contact, and then fell beside the log.

Preacher grabbed his arm in pain, but he never uttered a sound. He grimaced and held his wound as he kept his eyes on Clyde.

Now the pistol came quickly from behind the belt. Clyde aimed it straight toward Preacher's head.

"You're just asking for a bullet between the eyes Mister. I've shot men for no reason at all. Now you have the nerve to say such things to me. You just want a bullet to the brain, don't you?"

Preacher continued to stare at Clyde, as he rubbed his arm from the pain. Then he spoke but had no fear in his voice.

"You can try to destroy the truth Clyde. You can shoot me and anyone else that speaks the truth, but that won't destroy it. The truth is all around us and inside us. You spoke the truth just now. You've shot men for no reason. That same truth is what convicts you of the murders; because no man in his right mind asks for a bullet between the eyes. You've lived by the gun and I suspect you'll die by it."

Clyde cocked the pistol slowly. His hand trembled slightly as he aimed squarely for Preacher's head. At almost the same instant that he pulled the trigger, Clyde moved his aim to the bottle beside Preacher. As the loud gunshot rang out, glass sprayed onto Preacher and around him.

From the back of the car Bonnie jerked up as the gunshot startled her from sleep. She looked out to Clyde and then shouted in a hostile voice.

"Clyde, would you stop doing that? I told you it makes my whole body hurt." She then lay back down with a sound of exasperation.

Henry came running up with his pistol pulled. He looked at the shattered bottle and then Clyde who still held the pistol in the air. Sweat rolled down the side of his head. He slowly put the pistol back into his belt. He sneered at Preacher and turned away from him.

"We should probably be going." Henry said meekly.

Clyde cursed under his breath and went to the back of the car. He opened up the door and nudged Bonnie to get her to move over.

With Henry behind him Preacher went to the passenger side and climbed in, still holding his arm.

Henry gathered everything and stuffed it into the trunk. He quickly checked on Bonnie and Clyde in the back seat, then scanned the area for anything incidentally left behind. The young outlaw moved to the driver's side and climbed in; he started the car and they moved back onto the road.

An hour passed with no one in the car uttering a word.

Then a car came toward them. Dust floated around the back of it as it hurled into view. Police lights on top could be seen and as they passed each other while a sheriff insignia revealed itself on the side.

Clyde checked out the back window until the threat had gone far behind them. "How much longer till we reach your Pa's?"

Henry glanced in the rear-view mirror, and then answered Clyde. "A couple hours maybe, it's taking longer on these back roads."

"Find another place to stop. We'll stay off the roads a while and get back on the way before dark."

Henry nodded and began watching for a suitable spot to get off the road.

Soon he pulled the sedan onto an old road. An abandoned house came into view as the afternoon sun lay around the ramshackle home.

Henry stopped the car behind some trees. The doors opened and everyone began to exit the car.

Clyde helped Bonnie over to an area of the porch that hadn't yet broken down. He gently helped her sit and quickly lit a cigarette for her.

Henry and Preacher watched by the car and from a distance. Then Henry leaned back on the hood of the car.

"We'll be at my Pa's house in a few hours." Henry said this as he continued to watch Bonnie and Clyde. "Maybe he can figure something out. You're pushing your luck; you know that don't you?" Henry turned his head slightly toward Preacher; who glanced at Henry and then turned back to Bonnie and Clyde.

"Yeah, maybe your Pa can think of something. But I'm not figuring I'll make it out of this alive anymore." Preacher said as he briefly looked back at Henry. After this he sat down on the running board of the Ford.

Henry lit a cigarette and spewed a cloud of smoke from his mouth.

Clyde walked over to the car. "I'm going for a walk. Keep an eye on Bonnie." He spoke to Henry and never glanced at Preacher. He then walked with a slight limp to the road and soon disappeared from sight.

Henry looked at Preacher as if he should move, so Preacher stood up and began walking over to where Bonnie sat. Henry moved behind him.

Bonnie sat leaning against one of the corner beams. Preacher sat across from her on the ground. Henry remained standing. He smoked his cigarette and looked around nervously. Bonnie flicked her cigarette butt past Preacher.

"Give me another cigarette Henry."

He pulled one from his pack and after lighting it, handed it to Bonnie. She quickly took a long drag from it causing the tip to burn brighter. As Bonnie smoked her cigarette she stared blankly at Preacher.

Henry paced around the area and began to examine the broken-down house as a slight breeze moved through. He walked to the side and investigated a broken window. Then he moved to the back.

"Come here." Bonnie said flatly to Preacher.

Preacher looked at her with some apprehension. He slowly stood up and with his tattered coat in hand, moved closer to her.

"Sit down. I'm sure not going to stand to talk to you."

He did as Bonnie said and sat on the ground in front of her.

She took another long drag from the cigarette. Blowing the smoke out in an apparent feminine fashion she stared at Preacher. Then she sat up a little more and leaned over on her knees toward him.

"You know, I've never seen a man stand up to Clyde before." She said this with a sultry voice.

Preacher looked at Bonnie with compassion in his eyes but gave no reply. After a few seconds Bonnie continued.

"If a man were to come along that could stand up to Clyde, I just might be inclined to get away from this." She pulled another drag from the cigarette and blew the smoke into Preacher's face in a flirty manner. Then she smiled and turned her head a little. She gazed out at Preacher from the corner of her eyes.

He lowered his head when she blew the smoke in his face. He then looked at Bonnie again as she gazed at him seductively.

"Yeah, I might go with such a man and start fresh. I might even go to work again. You know I got a lot of tips when I worked as a waitress. I don't know that I would do that again; I hated it. But I might, if such a man were to come along." She then watched Preacher for his response.

A few long seconds passed by as Preacher seemed to consider what Bonnie had revealed to him. Then in a soft but firm tone he replied.

"You and Clyde are wanted dead or alive; but mostly dead Bonnie. They say you'll both be shot on sight the first chance the law gets. You're in fairly bad shape already. Your leg needs medical attention. You can't walk very far without someone's help. Do you really believe you can ever 'start fresh' again?"

Bonnie stared at Preacher with disdain. She appeared as if she were about to cry. Then slowly her face became stretched and lifeless. With a cold voice she began to speak begrudgingly, as if the words were struggling to get out.

"Get away from me. Get away from me right now. I don't want to ever speak to you again."

Preacher seemed saddened by this.

"Bonnie, it's the truth. I'm sorry, but it's the truth."

"Did you hear me? I said to get away from me. I don't want to hear anything you have to say." Now her voice became louder. "Get away from me!"

Preacher stood and walked back over to where he sat before just as Henry came around the corner of the house.

Henry looked at Bonnie curiously.

"Give me another cigarette Henry." She said.

He pulled a cigarette from his pack and quickly put it in her outstretched hand.

She instantly lit the cigarette from her previous one with a shaking hand and took a long and desperate drag from it. Then she looked back at Henry as the smoke expelled from her mouth and nostrils.

Henry seemed to wonder if she was all right but neither said anything.

Preacher sat with his legs crossed and laid his coat across his legs.

Soon Clyde came back and sat beside Bonnie. They all sat quietly as the cicadas screeched a constant tune in the trees around them. Henry found some cans of food in the car and they ate from the cans.

As the afternoon turned to evening, Clyde motioned for them to leave and soon the sedan was back on the road.

The sun dropped below the horizon as they pulled into the drive of Henry's father's house. Clyde walked around the car and just as Preacher began to get out he took hold of the door.

"Nope," he said as he lifted up a pair of handcuffs. He motioned for Preacher to move to the back seat behind the driver side, and then put one side on Preacher's wrist in the handcuffs and the other handcuff around the window frame of the car.

"I'm getting sick and tired of looking at you." He clicked the handcuffs closed on the door.

Preacher watched in silence as Clyde did this. But as Clyde began to walk away, Preacher replied. "You may not want to look at me anymore Clyde. But it won't change the fact that I'm here."

Clyde glanced back at Preacher but then quickly moved around to help Bonnie.

Henry's father appeared somewhat happy to see his son again. They all laughed about something as they went up the steps to the house.

Henry's father waited until the others were in. He then turned and looked out to where Preacher sat. He expressed concern as he stared in Preacher's direction. Then he turned back to the house and walked inside.

Outside, in the darkness, Preacher listened and stared at the dim light streaming from the windows. Laughter would erupt, and from the sounds and what little could be seen he determined they were playing cards and drinking.

He sat alone quietly. Clyde had done enough in restricting him from any interference. Apparently, he reminded them of things they wished to not think of.

He moved a little to get comfortable. The hours slowly slipped by. He placed his ragged coat behind his head and tried to rest.

Later, more laughter and noises of people walking out of the house aroused Preacher. Clyde and then Bonnie came out the door almost stumbling down the steps. Henry and his father walked out of the door behind them.

"Come on. I want to go for a drive. I'm sick of being in the house." Bonnie sounded about half intoxicated.

"That is a great idea Sugar." Clyde replied, not sounding very sober himself.

They moved toward the car and Preacher sat up. When Clyde reached the car he noticed Preacher and suddenly seemed to lose his humor.

Rather than helping Bonnie in the back he asked her if she would rather sit in the front for a while.

"Yeah, that sounds good. I'm getting tired of riding in the back anyway." After saying this Bonnie crawled into the front seat with Clyde's help.

Henry got into the driver's seat and started the car. Clyde unlocked Preacher and then shut his door, then walked around the back of the car and got in the back seat behind Bonnie and beside Preacher.

He looked over at Preacher with a foreboding in his eyes. Preacher pulled his coat from behind his neck and laid it across his legs.

As the sedan rumbled down the gravel roads Clyde would glance over at Preacher. As he pulled a drag from his cigarette, Clyde's face would light up enough to show an ominous expression. Then Bonnie would laugh about something and Clyde would temporarily turn his attention back to Bonnie.

As the night wore on Preacher pulled his coat up over him and leaned back in the corner between the door and the back seat. He closed his eyes as the others talked and drank.

Cigarette smoke swirled around his nose as all three outlaws smoked one cigarette after the other. He drifted into a light slumber and tried to find solace in the vibration of the car as he also attempted to tune out the loud criminals.

Sometime later, Preacher was aroused from his light sleep by the sudden jolt of the car. As he woke up he realized the vehicle must have hit a bump or pothole in the road.

A strange quiet inside the car indicated the three criminals had finally become exhausted. He laid his head back into the corner and glanced over to Clyde.

Clyde sat leaning in the opposite corner of the car in a similar fashion to Preacher. He stared at Preacher with an evil intent. In his hand he held his pistol pointed at Preacher. The rough road caused the barrel of the pistol to waver slightly, but Clyde sat silent, staunchly aiming it straight at Preacher.

He examined the situation while he lay in the corner. He said nothing but gazed into Clyde's eyes. The young outlaw appeared to be desperate and searching for something unseen.

Preacher knew there was little left to say to Clyde which he'd not already said. He waited and watched.

After what seemed to be many minutes, Clyde began to speak in a low and scornful voice.

"What am I to do about you? I thought if I brought you along, you might help us, but you're no good to me."

Preacher thought a few seconds before replying. Then he spoke in a calm tone.

"It's not my help you want Clyde. You want to manipulate me. You want me to present something false in order to help you justify your actions. Regardless of what you decide to do about me. I won't be beaten down and turned into a living lie."

Clyde now appeared to consider the words before replying, "If you got no use for me, then I got no concern about you."

"There's still time Clyde."

The outlaw seemed puzzled by Preacher's words.

"Time for what?"

"Time to do the right thing," Preacher replied.

This only seemed to anger Clyde even more. He turned slightly to speak to Henry.

"What time is it, Henry?"

Henry acknowledged Clyde's question by a nod. He pulled a cigarette lighter from his jacket pocket and lit it. Then he held it over his watch as he tried to check the time and steer the car. After a few seconds of glancing at his watch Henry answered Clyde.

"It's twelve minutes till midnight."

Clyde looked back at Preacher. He cocked the hammer of the pistol back.

"There's no more time." Clyde pulled the trigger.

The inside of the car lit up as the loud gunshot rang out. The car slid to a halt as Henry slammed on the breaks. Bonnie awoke in a shock and sat up quickly. After realizing they were not being shot at, she instantly became angry.

"Clyde... how many times do I have to tell you to quit that? It makes my leg hurt!"

The back door opened, and Preacher fell limp from the car; rolling into the ditch. The door slammed shut and the car sped away into the darkness.

Dawn broke slowly over the horizon and as the warm sun rose higher into the sky a snake crawled cautiously alongside the road and past the motionless body in the ditch. Cicadas began screeching, individually at first, until slowly a chorus of their strange calls erupted in the trees.

Preacher stirred. Slowly he picked himself up. Sitting in the ditch he looked down and carefully examined himself for damage.

He then examined the ragged coat that he had over him when Clyde pulled the trigger. Lifting it up he identified a bullet entrance on one side and the exit on the other side; indicating a bullet passing through the coat but somehow missing him.

After studying his coat, Preacher moved a little farther from the ditch and closer to the cooler shade of a nearby tree. He sat staring out at the barren road. The cicadas became even louder as the sun crept higher into the sky. Still Preacher sat silently staring at the road.

The sun overhead indicated a time of around 10:00 am and the cicadas now screeched with an unrelenting roar of sound. The road silently mocked Preacher as nothing and no one crossed it all morning.

Then, with a shocking urgency the cicadas fell silent.

Nothing could be heard. The slight breeze seemed to have also died.

Preacher gazed around but made no move. The eerie silence held true as seconds ticked by.

Then, he slowly stood up and walked to the side of the dusty road. With the battered coat on his arm he put his hands into his pockets and turned to stare down the rugged gravel lane.

Now the cicadas slowly began to screech again. The breeze once again floated slowly through the air and the leaves in the trees fluttered about in a carefree manner.

After a few moments, the sound of a car could be heard. Then it came into view. Preacher watched as it approached. It swerved a little from one side of the road to the other. He stood fast by the road, not moving.

The automobile passed by him and slowed down. Again, it swerved and after traveling about a quarter mile the car suddenly slid to a stop beside the road.

Preacher turned and began walking toward the vehicle.

The door opened and a large man in a white suit slid halfway out of the car. As Preacher got closer, he watched him with interest.

The man held his chest while leaning over, obviously laboring for breath. He stared at the ground between his feet as he held the place on his chest where his heart would be.

Preacher approached the man and could see he was sweating profusely.

"Are you all right?"

The man turned to Preacher with a taut red face and fear still stretched across it. He then moved his hand inside his suit pocket and pulled out a handkerchief as if in an effort to hide the fact he was holding his chest. He wiped his face gingerly with the handkerchief.

"Yeah, I'm fine."

The man stood with some effort. He leaned on the car and tried to pull himself together.

"It's fiercely hot. I just needed to catch my breath."

Preacher studied the man who appeared to be in his late fifties.

"You headed this way?" The man asked this with a feeble point from his hand.

"Yes, I'm headed that way."

"Come on then. There's no need for you to be out here in the heat, all alone like an orphan."

After saying this he chuckled a little and got back into the driver's seat.

Preacher walked around and climbed into the passenger seat across from the man.

As the car began to move down the road Preacher sat watching the man in a concerned manner as he wiped his forehead often with the handkerchief.

Initially he paid little attention to Preacher. Then, as time went by he seemed to feel better. After a while he started to talk.

"This heat reminds me of a week I spent in New Orleans." He looked over at Preacher and smiled, then continued.

"We had a meeting back in, oh 1920 I believe it was. My partner wanted to go to the Red-Light district. He says to me, 'Leonard, we need to go get us a city woman for the night. The wives will never know a thing.'" Then Leonard laughed and looked at Preacher slyly.

"So, we went to the Red Light district and let me tell you, I got hold of a sweet young whore. She said she was twenty-one. But I don't think she could have been over seventeen!" He laughed again.

"She wasn't so sweet when I got done with her though!" He smiled as if reminiscing and then wiped the sweat from his brow as he glanced over at Preacher.

Preacher gave no expression as he simply sat listening to Leonard, who now appeared very excited to speak his mind.

As the car rolled down the dusty roads Leonard became more revealing and he confessed with zeal many things to Preacher.

"And he hung in that tree for three days before any of them blacks were brave enough to cut him down. I know for sure, because I went by and checked. You see that's what the Klan is there for; to make sure they don't get too high and mighty."

Leonard expressed pride in the dark things he disclosed to Preacher.

As he spoke, Preacher listened intently but gave no sign of approval nor disapproval. This in turn appeared to make Leonard feel at ease because Preacher didn't object to his deeds.

An hour passed by and Leonard had spoken almost without ceasing the entire time.

Then, they suddenly came upon a mass of cars pulled over to the side of the road. People walked toward something ahead and a few were walking away from the mysterious attraction.

Leonard slowed down and pulled over to the side.

"What in H E double L?" He said this with astonishment as people moved by his window.

When a man passed by in the opposite direction as if he had already seen what lay ahead, Leonard asked him. "What's going on up there?"

The man stopped and moved closer to Leonard's window.

"They gunned down Bonnie and Clyde up the road a bit. The law caught 'em in an ambush. A sheriff and some deputies must have plugged 'em a thousand times. There's blood everywhere. It is like a slaughterhouse!"

When the man said this Leonard immediately became excited and a smile erupted across his face.

"You don't say, Bonnie and Clyde? I've got to see this."

The man shook his head a little as if feeling ill. "It's a bloody mess. I ain't ever seen anything like it." He then left in the direction he was going before Leonard stopped him.

Leonard opened the door and got out. He looked over to the passenger seat with an anxious expression.

"Ain't you coming to see?"

Preacher said nothing for a few seconds, and then shook his head with an expression of sadness indicating he didn't intend on going.

"Don't you want to see this?" Leonard asked again with some bewilderment.

"Why would any decent person be eager to see such a thing Leonard?"

The smile faded as Leonard considered this. "Well, this is Bonnie and Clyde though; the outlaws."

Preacher stared at Leonard a few seconds.

"They were still human beings."

Now Leonard's eyes dropped as he seemed to be searching for something else. His face twisted a little as he appeared to see something inside himself that was unattractive.

He looked briefly back to the passenger's seat.

"Well, the truth is, I don't ordinarily like to see this sort of stuff. It's not that I enjoy other people's pain."

Preacher looked him straight into the eyes and the two men remained in this state briefly before Preacher finally spoke.

"Is that the truth, Leonard? Is that the real truth?"

Leonard expressed shame on his face now. He turned away from Preacher and stared at the ground briefly. Yet he gave no answer. He then slowly closed the car door and turned to join the mass of people.

Preacher sat alone, as the multitude moved eagerly to the place of the dead.

The End

We hope you enjoyed The House on Cooper Lane and Twelve Minutes till Midnight. You may also be interested in Ever the Wayward Sky by Oliver Phipps. For your convenience we've added a preview of Ever the Wayward Sky and listed some of his other works here.

EVER THE WAYWARD SKY

Oliver Phipps

Chapter One:

THE WAR IS OVER, BUT THERE'S NO END IN SIGHT

A light haze lay over the North Carolina ground. Sergeant James Taft stepped out of an officer's tent.

"Yes Sir, I will, first thing this afternoon." He replied while moving from the entrance.

As soon as he was completely outside, he became aware of something unusual. The low sound of cheering began to erupt on the far side of the camp. Sergeant Taft turned toward the strange sounds just as his lieutenant stepped out from the tent behind him.

Both men were around the same height and build; five foot ten inches, more or less. However, Sergeant Taft had short dark hair that wasn't curly and unruly as the lieutenants' was. And, James also wore a mustache and goatee, which was popular among the Union cavalrymen.

"What's going on, Sergeant?" The lieutenant moved up beside James, and both watched as a spontaneous celebration appeared to be overtaking the entire camp.

"I don't know, Sir. But it seems to be moving this way." As Sergeant Taft said this, soldiers walked at a rapid pace closer to the two men. They yelled and shouted along the way. One man came swiftly toward them, waving his hat and cheering loudly.

"What's going on soldier?" The lieutenant asked when the man came closer.

"Lee surrendered, Sir. He surrendered to General Grant." Then the man jogged away, shouting and jumping as he went.

The lieutenant looked at Sergeant Taft, who looked back at him. They both seemed to be in disbelief. Then, as more and more soldiers came running through the camp shouting, both men began to smile. They turned and shook hands; congratulating each other for surviving.

James Taft had seldom thought or believed the war would end. After more than four years of fighting, he had a difficult time accepting this reality. As the next few weeks went by, however, the twenty-three-year-old sergeant began to accept that he had indeed survived the war.

Eventually, his unit, the 9th Pennsylvania cavalry began to muster out in Kentucky.

"What are you going to do now, Sergeant?" A young private asked James as they left the headquarters building. Sergeant Taft examined his discharge papers. He seemed to be a bit confused and disoriented.

"I'm not sure, private."

"You're not sure? Ain't you going home, sergeant?"

"I suppose I will. What are you going to do?"

The private laughed. "Oh, I got so many things I'm going to do! The first thing is, I'm going to marry my sweetheart, Dolly. Oh, she is a beauty! You got a sweetheart, Sergeant?"

James glanced at the young man.

"No, I don't suppose that I do, Private."

The young man laughed again. "You should get you a sweetheart."

The man stayed with James as they turned in gear and finished other various tasks to complete their discharge. He spoke with almost no restraint. James didn't care though as his mind was absent of anything to talk about.

He felt lost as he said goodbye to his horse. He felt naked as he turned in his revolver and rifle. The saber he'd bought with his money, he gladly packed it with his other meager belongings.

James couldn't seem to break away from the numbness that had taken over him. During his trip home to Pennsylvania, he again became lost in thought. He remembered those he knew that had died in battle. He considered the men he had killed in combat. They wouldn't be going home, ever. They still lay on the battlefield in the cold earth. The war was over. Why couldn't he be glad like so many others? Why did he feel that he shouldn't be leaving the army and yet at the same time, feel that he could not endure any more of the savage brutality he had gone through for four and a half years?

His hometown presented a celebratory atmosphere as James stepped off the train. Banners were hung all around, welcoming the victorious soldier's home.

"James, James Taft! Welcome, home James! My, my, I barely recognized you. You were, what, eighteen when you enlisted? You've grown into quite the man, and hero for that matter."

"Thank you, Mr. Carleton." James shook the man's outstretched hand as a small band struck up the Battle Cry of Freedom. A few of the town women handed out baked items, and one of them poured a cup of black coffee for him.

He looked over the small train station as he sipped the coffee. It hadn't changed much over the years. Yet everything seemed different now.

An elderly lady approached him.

"Your mama is going to be so happy to see you, James! She came down here several times hoping you would arrive with some of the other boys that were coming home. But you've all been coming home a few at a time now after the main group returned."

James smiled at the woman; she had aged considerably in appearance since he last saw her.

"Yes Mrs. Johnson, the cavalry had some extended duties to perform. It took a bit longer for us to muster out."

"Well, no matter. I know she'll be very happy to see you. We're all so proud of you boys."

Mrs. Johnson then took her small handkerchief and put it close to her eye. "It's just a shame we lost so many good young men to that," she acted as if she wanted to say something else, but then continued, "that, terrible war."

James tried to sound compassionate. "Yes Mrs. Johnson, I agree."

"Well James, you tell your mother and the rest of your family hello for me. And we're just so glad to have you back."

Mrs. Johnson then went to speak with another soldier that had also returned on the train.

James moved out of the station and began walking through the Pennsylvania town that he'd grown up in. Memories rushed back to him as he passed buildings and landmarks. Some of the memories brought feelings of his father, who had died when James was only fourteen.

"James? It surely is young James Taft!" An elderly man in an old suit came up quickly to him with an excited expression on his face.

"Hello, Dr. Weston," James said with not nearly as much excitement as he shook the extended doctors' hand.

"James, it is so good to have you back. I'm sorry you didn't get the big parade and all. We had a big to do when our boys from the regiment returned. I wish you could have come home to that."

"It's alright Doc. Mr. Carleton and some of the ladies met us at the station."

"Well, that's good, James. We've tried to have someone at the station as you boys continue to come in."

"I believe we'll be some of the last, Doc," James replied.

The doctor looked down and shook his head a little. "It seems we've lost so many." Then he glanced back up to James. "Do you need a ride out to your place? I can have the horses hooked up to my carriage."

James smiled. "Thank you, Doc, but I would like to walk. I could use a good long stroll."

"Alright James, I understand."

As he moved on out of town and toward his boyhood home, a dark feeling came over him. He gazed over at the "swimming hole" that he and his brother John had swum many times in. Now the laughter he remembered seemed so far away. His heart felt as if it could no longer recover such a joyful time. The death he had seen and dealt with now anchored him to a place neither high nor low. He simply existed.

He continued toward the family home and memories fluttered through his mind. Races with his brother and friends; some of whom now lay buried in the earth of a distant battlefield. Still, James couldn't shake off the darkness to receive the warm thoughts he desired. Maybe, the sight of his home and his mother would stir the embers of joy that he hoped were still in his heart, somewhere.

Slowly the two-story house came into view. As James moved closer, he became frightened. He slowed down and felt a sense of dread. How could a man who had been in more battles than he could recall be terrified of returning home?

James stopped. He stood at a distance from the house. As his heart raced, his mind struggled for an answer. Slowly, the problem began to unravel as he searched his very soul. The questions revealed their ugly presence in his thoughts.

Would they see the terrible things? Would his mother sense the blood and death on him? Would his nephew and niece feel the heat of the hell he had passed through, time and time again? Surely, they would know. He started walking again but felt the weight of these concerns with every step he took. Sweat dripped along the side of his head as these thoughts entrenched themselves into his fears.

With the reluctance, he had felt before racing into a battle, James forced himself to continue moving forward. The aging house came into view as did his niece who was outside. She had grown much since the last time he had seen her. The years had changed her dramatically from the four-year-old girl he remembered. She had her back to him and was kneeled over, picking wildflowers.

James stood outside the small wooden fence that was in obvious need of repairs. He watched his niece in silence as she hummed and picked the flowers one by one. He felt himself trembling in anticipation of her noticing him. Would she scream in fear? Would she see the things he had been through and cry from sadness?

He wanted to do something to let her know that he was behind her, but he felt too frightened to do anything. Then, as she turned, she noticed him standing outside the fence. She stared at him for several seconds with a slightly startled expression. James smiled a little smile at her.

"Uncle James?" She took several small steps toward him as she asked this.

"Hello, Grace." He said to her, relieved that she couldn't see the wariness inside him.

Grace cautiously walked over to the fence. She then extended her handful of flowers to him. James took the flowers and softly said. "Thank you."

"We've been waiting for you Uncle James." As she said this, James' mother stepped out to the front porch and immediately put her hand to her mouth and began to weep.

"James...!" She moved quickly down the porch toward him. His brother now came out and then his wife, with their son behind her. All of them began to say his name and rush to hug him.

Later, he sat in the main room. Everyone sat around him as if he was about to tell a grand tale. His sister-in-law brought him a drink.

"We've been hoping you would show up any day now James." His brother John said and then continued.

"Ma waited at the train station again and again when the regiment began to arrive, but no one could tell us anything about the 9th. We finally stopped going to the station. No one seemed to know anything about the cavalry."

James took a drink and sat the glass on a table beside him.

"Well, we had some extra duties to take care of. We watched over some of the larger reb units as they surrendered. I didn't know how long it would be or I would have written and let everyone know."

His mother appeared to glow from joy.

"No matter, James. We're just so happy to have you back, son."

"Yeah, James, we'll get this place back into shape in no time with you back!" His brother John added.

James smiled a little. He felt strangely out of place sitting peacefully with his family.

"Yeah, we'll do that John." He picked up his drink, more from being nervous than needing it.

As he took a sip, his mind searched for the reason he felt so uncomfortable. He didn't want to talk about farming. He didn't want to think about getting the place back into shape. He felt depressed even considering these things.

Then, with no warning, his nephew Johnny unexpectedly asked a question.

"Did you kill a bunch of Reb's Uncle James?"

John immediately reprimanded his son as everyone looked around in shock.

"Johnny, don't ask such a thing!"

"Why Pa, I want to know?"

A strange sensation swept over James, and he had to get up. He then replied with obvious discomfort, "That's alright, John... I think I'll get some air for a few minutes."

He left the room as the others tried to explain to young Johnny why he shouldn't ask such questions. James stepped out onto the porch and sat down on the steps, in the dark.

His heart beat rapidly. He realized something terrible now. Only when Johnny asked him that question did he feel alive again. What was wrong with him? He ran his fingers through his hair.

John stepped out on the porch behind him. He sat down beside his younger brother.

"I'm sorry James. He's just... so young."

"No, it's alright. I just needed some air. I'm not used to being inside. We slept under the stars as much as we did anywhere else."

John glanced over at his brother. He took a deep breath of the moist night air.

"I wanted to join up, but with Pa gone and two young children."

"No... John. You did the right thing. You're the real soldier for taking care of Ma and this place. I'm sorry that I ran off and left you like I did. I had visions of being some hero, I suppose."

The two men sat quietly for a few minutes and stared out over the dark fields in front of them. Then John said with a softened voice.

"Sounds like your unit had it pretty rough. Up against Forrest and Morgan, seems the 9th took on some of the toughest."

"Yeah, I guess we got our share of it," James replied.

"Well, at least you didn't leave anything out there on the battlefield." John then slapped James on the leg. He stood up and walked back into the house. James then said in a small voice, to himself.

"I'm not so sure of that."

As the days passed, James felt himself sinking further into depression. He tried to work on the family farm but couldn't focus on the tasks. Darkness slowly began to swallow him from the inside out.

"Well, we finally pulled that old stump out of the South field." John attempted to sound encouraging at the dinner table.

"That's wonderful. That old tree always irritated your Pa.

I'm glad we took care of it, and it's gone for good." His mother glanced over at James after saying this.

Her son sat staring blankly at his plate of food. He heard nothing they had said.

His mother turned and looked across the table at John, who then glanced over at his wife, Velma. All three now watched James as he held his fork over his food and appeared to be far away.

The two children took notice of what was occurring and began watching their Uncle also.

Realizing the children were watching, Velma stood up and took a pitcher of water over to James.

"Would you like some more water, James?"

He almost shook as he came out of the apparent trance.

"Oh, no Velma, thank you."

Johnny laughed a little, and this caused Grace to giggle as well.

"You children eat now. No playing."

"Yes, Grandma." Both children replied, almost in unison.

James looked around the table with a lost expression on his face.

"I think it'll rain tonight," John said to bring supper back on track. "What do you think James?"

"Yes, it might."

He knew something wasn't right. He realized now that he'd been somewhere else. He didn't know what to do about it, though. He glanced around at his family. He loved them dearly, but he didn't belong here. He wasn't sure where he belonged, but he knew now that it wasn't here.

Later, as James lay down to sleep, the rain began. The soft pattering of raindrops outside his window caused a soothing effect, and he drifted into sleep. Then the thunder came, and as James slipped farther into slumber, he found himself on a faraway battlefield again. As the sounds of the storm erupted outside, the cannons roared on the battlefield of James' dream.

"I heard them was Morgan's boys over there, Sergeant."

A young private nervously spoke to Sergeant Taft, who was riding back and forth in front of the men. James reined his horse in to answer the young cavalryman.

"Don't matter who they are, private! That cavalry unit is protecting the Reb's flank, and we'll run them off the battlefield, or die trying!"

When James said this, the private appeared to calm down. But he was still obviously frightened. All the soldiers appeared concerned. The horses moved underneath them nervously; sensing death to be close at hand. Smoke from the guns drifted through the unit's ranks as James scanned the faces of his men.

He then moved closer to the young private. James thought he might be able to say something to calm the young man, but as he came near, the soldier began to speak.

"I sure got the feeling that I'm going to be one of those that die trying, Sergeant. You ever get that feeling?"

James reined in his mount again, trying to calm it. The horse quivered under him in an apprehensive excitement for the battle at hand. Then, James lied to the young private. He always lied in these situations.

"Almost every day, private." After James had said this, the man calmed some more. He smiled a little. James smiled slightly as well, and then he thought of several other men that had told him the same sort of thing over the years. They all died on the battlefield after telling him this. The cracking of rifle and cannon fire became intense. He positioned his horse to the front of the unit, ready for battle.

Their lieutenant rode swiftly up from the back of the unit.

"Alright boys, it's time, let's give'em hell."

The lieutenant then pulled his saber out and nodded to their bugler, who immediately sounded the charge. Sergeant Taft spurred his horse just as the lieutenant charged forward.

"Let's go 9th," James yelled out, and his heart began to pound inside his chest.

The ground began to tremble as the horses burst into a gallop.

James looked across the field at the enemy just as bullets began to sing around him.

He became hot as the blood rushed to his head. Then, as always, he slowly became numb as the specter of death approached.

He put the reins in his mouth and lowered his head as if facing a fierce wind. He could now see the enemy's faces clearly.

As the gap closed, he pulled his saber out with his left hand and his revolver out with his right.

The famed "Rebel yell" could be heard from the opposing forces, sending chills down his back.

Now everything began to happen at lightning speed. The two cavalry units collided with the ferocity of a train wreck. As he moved into the Confederates' ranks, he swung his razor-sharp saber and took a Rebels' head almost entirely off from the shoulders. He then turned to his left and fired his pistol into the chest of another, removing the man from his horse in the process.

The sound of bullets flying by him mixed with bodies being struck and cries of pain, all mingled with anger, leather, and metal striking metal.

Another rebel rode up to his right. He was young, and James could see the fear in his eyes. He fired his pistol, but James anticipated it just in time to move. The bullet whizzed by so close that he felt the heat. He maneuvered his saber as the young soldier attempted to cock his pistol again. He lunged the blade forward and felt the steel sink into the man's body. He watched briefly as the soldier realized James had just ended his life.

He pulled the blade from the man and turned to his left as another soldier was about to fire his rifle at him. James quickly aimed and instinctively fired his cocked pistol. The soldier leaned back as the bullet hit him, firing the gun into the air before falling from his horse.

The enemy was all around him now. He shot another Rebel from his horse. Another one rode toward him as if to avenge his comrade. James shot him also as he tried to swing his saber.

He wanted to get out of the enclosed fighting. He maneuvered his mount to the right, then ran another rebel through the back with his saber. He struggled to pull the blade free as the soldier fell backward onto it.

A bullet cut through the side of his coat contacting his flesh. He remained on top of his horse. He spotted the enemy that fired the shot. He aimed his revolver and shot as the soldier tried to shoot again. James' shot almost removed the soldier's head.

He pressed his right arm against the wounded side as the pain came. Angered, he spurred his horse forward. He swung his blade and the contact nearly took a passing rebel's arm off.

Another rebel rode toward him at a furious pace, seeming ready to take James down with his saber. James lifted his pistol and shot him from his horse. Then he immediately ran his blade into the side of another rebel that had moved close to him.

James sensed another enemy soldier taking aim; the shot intended for the young private he had spoken with before the start of the battle. James lifted his pistol and pulled the trigger. The clicking of an empty revolver was all he heard. As the young private turned, he would see the bullet from the enemy that would kill him. James yelled out.

"Noooo...!!"

He cocked the pistol again as the rebel fired. The young private jerked back as the bullet slammed into his chest. James again pulled the trigger; again, and again, the clicking of an empty pistol.

"James?"

The Rebel then turned toward him, and everything slowed

down. James raised his saber as the hot blood flowed to his head and caused a flash of anger inside him.

"James, are you alright?"

The battlefield began to fade. James slowly saw his room by the light of a lamp that his mother held. He found himself sitting on the edge of his bed. His left arm raised as if he were holding a saber, while his right arm was elevated halfway and pointed from his body in a manner suggesting a pistol ready to be used.

He blinked several times and looked to his mother, who stood in the doorway with a lamp. She appeared very concerned. Then, John stepped up behind her. As James lowered his arms, Grace and Johnny stepped to the door to see what the commotion was. At last, Velma stepped to the door behind John.

"I guess I was dreaming. I'm sorry if I disturbed anyone."

"Come on children; Uncle James just had a dream." His mother attempted to usher the children away from the doorway. John seemed to want to say something but couldn't find the words. Velma turned and went back toward their bedroom. Finally, John spoke in a nervous tone.

"Well, good night James. I'll uh... I'll see you at breakfast." he then waved slightly and left for his bedroom.

James sat in silence on the edge of the bed. His heart continued to race long after everyone had settled back into their beds. He told himself that he hated the battlefield. The smell of smoke and blood still permeated his nostrils, even though it was only a dream. And yet here he sat, on the edge of the bed, in darkness and silence, reliving the vivid dream over and over in his mind. He wanted to be there again, and this frightened him more than any battle ever did.

As the morning light slowly peeked over the horizon, James' mother stepped out onto the porch where her son sat in a weathered chair. He gazed out to the horizon and only glanced away as his mother sat down across from him.

Several minutes had passed before either spoke. His mother began, softly, but seeming to struggle for her words.

"I wish... well, I just wish your father were here, James. He would be so much better with something like this."

James glanced at her and smiled a little. He then turned back to watch the morning sun creeping up. After a few seconds, he spoke with a slow but resolved tone.

"I never really thought about what I would do after the war, Ma. Because I never believed, I would live through it." He paused and his mother looked down a little as if his words pained her some. He then continued with the same tone.

"I can't stay here. This... staying in one place, it's doing something to me. I'm not for certain what, but it's not good, I know that."

His mother continued to gaze down at the porch, appearing to almost cry. After several seconds, she straightened and again spoke softly.

"You shouldn't run from your problems, Son."

He turned to his mother and examined her face. He loved her so much and wanted to make her understand that he had no desire to leave. He tried desperately to find the words. She looked back to her son with a hope that he might be able to stay. But as she gazed into his eyes, James realized what he needed to say.

"I'm not running from them, Ma. I've got to charge them, at full gallop. It's the only thing I know how to do now. I've got to meet them out there... somewhere, and overcome them, or die trying. I don't know what the outcome will be, but I know now what happens if I stay here."

A tear ran down his mother's face as she realized his words were true, and she would once again be losing her son. She put her head down and wiped the tear away. She nodded a little as another tear dropped to her lap.

Later that morning, John approached his brother, who had walked to the creek. James sat on a large rock, the same one the two had used as young boys to jump into the water.

"It's been a long time since you and I went swimming here." John then sat down beside his brother.

James turned and glanced at him. He then looked back to the creek and tossed a small stone in, as if he'd been waiting for a reason to throw it into the water.

"Yeah, feels like a different lifetime. I've been thinking about those days; before..." James acted reluctant to even say the word.

"Before the war..." John said, with the tone of a big brother. He obviously wanted to confront the problem and resolve it.

James sensed this, but knew the problem was not as simple as removing a tree stump.

"Yeah, before the war," he replied without looking up.

Again, the silence prevailed and the soft flowing creek, along with a few birds was the only sounds heard. Finally, John felt the need to say something.

"Ma says you're going to leave?"

James reached down and picked up another small stone, then replied.

"I can't stay here any longer, John. The war did something to me. I don't know what, exactly, but I know I've got to move. If I don't, I'll get sick."

John looked over at his brother and tried to find an answer. He could think of nothing to change his brother's mind. With no solution in sight, he decided to do what he could to be a friend.

"Where are you planning on going to?"

James glanced at John and felt glad his brother was trying to understand. He tossed the small stone into the creek.

"West, there's a lot of room to move around, out that way. I saved most of my pay from the Army, so I should have enough to get me by for a while. I'll give Ma some money before I leave. I know it won't be the same as having an extra hand around, but maybe it'll help some."

John could only nod in agreement. He knew his brother would stay if he were able to. He patted James' leg and stood up.

"Will you be coming to dinner?"

"Yeah, I'll be back later, before dinner."

John nodded and began walking back toward the house. James again stared at the creek, as if it might answer some of the questions in his mind.

As the sun crept up toward noon, James left the small waterway and went back to the house. He decided he would leave as soon as he could get a good horse and the proper equipment together for an extended trip out West.

Over the next several days he purchased a good mount and all the necessary gear, including two brand new Colt Army revolvers and a Henry rifle.

The departure day came, and he said his good-byes, then moved down the road, away from the house where he had grown to be a young man.

Upon reaching the creek, he turned the horse around and looked back at his home in the distance. He didn't want to leave it. But in his heart, James knew he had to. Something inside him would not rest. The battle within had to run its course, somewhere and somehow. Staying here would only worsen the situation and disrupt the family he loved. With this thought in mind, he turned his horse and moved down the road, toward the struggle he knew he must face. Out there, in the West, somewhere, an unseen enemy awaited him.

*

Thank you for reading the preview of Ever the Wayward Sky. Here are some other books by Oliver Phipps that you may be interested in.

Sane Grace

In the year 2054, earth has become an inter-galactic outpost for trade among friendly planets.

The potential rewards in this new era are great, but so are the risks. An alien drug called Fellirex has recently saturated the black market. It's cheap and highly addictive, and in few weeks, half the world's population could become addicts.

From across the globe, the world's finest are gathered to end the smuggling of this drug. Lieutenant Wolfe, a young and attractive special operations officer, seems completely out of place among the heroes and decorated veterans.

Much to the frustration of her commanding officer, she is given an assignment, and her teammate is almost immediately, critically wounded. A detective takes a chance and volunteers to team up with the seemly erratic young woman. However, it is not long before he questions that decision.

Trapped on a wild and hazardous journey across the globe and into space itself, the detective realizes Grace may not be who he thought she was. In fact, Grace herself appears to question her true intentions and motives.

A Tempest Soul

Seventeen-year-old Gina Falcone has been alone for most of her life. Her father passed away while she was young, and her un-affectionate mother eventually leaves her to care for herself when she was only thirteen.

Though her epic journey begins by an almost deadly mistake, Gina will find many of her hearts desires in the most unlikely of places. The loss of everything is the catalyst that brings her to an unimagined level of accomplishment in her life.

However, Gina, soon realizes it is the same events that brought her success that may also bring everything crashing down around her. The new life she has built soon beckons for something she left behind. Now, the new woman must find a way to dance through a life she could have never dreamt of.

Where the Strangers Live

When a passenger plane disappeared over the Indian Ocean in autumn 2013, a massive search gets underway.

A deep trolling, unmanned pod picks up faint readings, and soon the deep-sea submersible Oceana and her three crew members are four miles below the ocean surface in search of the black box from flight N340.

Nothing could have prepared the submersible crew for what they discover and what happens afterward. Ancient evils and other world creatures challenge the survival of the Oceana's crew. Mysteries of the past are revealed, and death hangs in the balance for Sophie, Troy and Eliot in this deep-sea Science Fiction thriller.

Twelve Minutes till Midnight

A man catches a ride on a dusty Louisiana road, only to find out he's traveling with notorious outlaws Bonnie and Clyde.

The suspense is nonstop as confrontation settles in, between a man determined to stand on truth, and an outlaw determined to dislocate him from it.

"Twelve Minutes till Midnight will take you on an unforgettable ride."

Diver Creed Station

Wars, diseases, and a massive collapse of civilization have ravaged the human-race of a hundred years in the future. Finally, in the late twenty-second century, mankind slowly begins to struggle back from the edge of extinction.

When a huge "virtual life" facility is restored from a hibernation type of storage and slowly brought back online, a new hope materializes.

Fragments of humanity begin to move into the remnants of Denver and the Virtua-Gauge facilities, which offer seven days of virtual leisure for seven days work in this new and growing social structure.

Most inhabitants of this new lifestyle begin to hate the real world, and work for the seven-day period inside the virtual pods. It's the variety of luxury role play inside the virtual zone that supply's the incentive needed to work hard for seven days in the real world.

In this new social structure, a man can work for seven days in a food dispersal unit, and earn seven days as a twenty-first century software billionaire in the virtual zone. As time goes by, and more of the virtual pods are brought back online life appears to be getting better.

Rizette and her husband Oray are young technicians that settle into their still-new marriage as the virtual facilities expand and thrive.

Oray has recently attained the level of a Class A Diver and enjoys his job. The Divers are skilled technicians that perform critical repairs to the complex system, from inside the virtual zone.

His occupation as a Diver demands constant work in the secure "lower levels" of the system. These highly secure areas are the dividing space between the real world and the world of the virtual zone. When the facility was built, the original designers intentionally placed this buffer zone in the programming to avoid threats from non-living virtual personnel.

As Oray becomes more experienced in his elite technical position as a Diver, he is approached by his virtual assistant and forced to make a difficult decision. Oray's decision triggers events that soon pull him and his wife Rizette into a deadly quest for survival.

The stage becomes a massive and complex maze of virtual world sequences, as escape or entrapment hang on precious threads of information.

System ghosts from the distant past, intermingle with mysterious factions that have thrown Oray and Rizette into a cyberspace trap with little hope for survival.

Ghosts of Company K:
Based on a True Story

Tag along with young Bud Fisher during his daily adventures in this ghostly tale based on actual events. It's 1971 and Bud and his family move into an old house in Northern Arkansas. Bud soon discovers they live not far from a very interesting cave and a historic Civil War battle site. As odd things start to happen, Bud tries to solve the mysteries, but soon the entire family experiences a haunting situation.

If you enjoy ghost tales based on true events, then you'll enjoy Ghosts of Company K. This heartwarming story brings the reader into the life and experiences of a young boy growing up in the early 1970s. Seen through innocent and unsuspecting eyes, Ghosts of Company K reveals a haunting tale from the often-unseen perspective of a young boy.

Bane of the Innocent

"There's no reason for them to shoot us; we ain't anyone" - Sammy, Bane of the Innocent.

Two young boys become unlikely companions during the fall of Atlanta. Sammy and Ben somehow find themselves, and each other, in the rapidly changing and chaotic environment of the war-torn Georgia City.

As the siege ends and the fall begins in late August and early September of 1864, the Confederate troops begin to move out, and Union forces cautiously move into the city. Ben and Sammy simply struggle to survive, but in the process, they develop a friendship that will prove more important than either could imagine.

A Life Naïve

Life for twenty-seven-year-old Hershel Lawson has been relatively uneventful, and that's the way he likes it. When his grandmother passes away, leaving him her car and a last wish of him taking her ashes to L.A., his life takes a turn and it will never be the same again.

With his new task and grandmother's ashes, Hershel sets out from St. Louis Missouri in the spring of 1962. He travels unimpeded along scenic Route 66 for two days, but is suddenly and unexpectedly relieved of two important things, his car and wallet.

Sally is a sassy and street-smart young woman on her way to Hollywood. She's determined to prove everyone wrong in the "one horse town" she left and be successful as an actress in California. Through mishaps of her own, Sally comes across Hershel. Though neither one realizes it, the real journey is about to begin.

Take a seat and journey with Hershel and Sally along historic Route 66 during its heyday. Laugh and maybe shed a tear or two as they struggle against the odds, and often each other, to make it a few more miles down the highway.

The Bitter Harvest

It's 1825, and a small Native American village has lost many of its people and bravest warriors to a pack of Lofa; huge beasts' humanoid in shape and covered with coarse hair. The creatures are taller than any normal man, and fiercer than even the wildest animal.

Rather than leave the land of their ancestors, the tribe chooses to stay and fight the beasts. But they're losing the war, and perhaps more critically, they're almost without hope.

The small community grasps for anything to help them survive. There is a warrior on the frontier known as Orenda. He's already legendary across the west for his bravery and honor.

Onsi, a young villager, sets out on a journey to find the warrior.

Orenda will be forced to choose between almost certain death, not just for himself, but also his warrior wife Nazshoni and her brother Kanuna, or a dishonorable refusal that would mean annihilation for the entire village.

The crucial decision is only the beginning, and Orenda will soon face the greatest test of his life; the challenge that could turn out to be too much even for a legendary warrior.

Into the Crimson Mist

From the tales of Orenda, book two. This is the sequel to The Bitter Harvest.

After a long winter encampment, Orenda, Nazshoni, Kanuna and Onsi cross the Mississippi river and venture west. Their destination is far and Orenda intends to move the small group of warriors with haste in the hope of reaching an embattled tribe far to the west of the great river.

The plan begins to unravel when they come across a ghost village and then dire forebodings from an old Shaman. There is a shapeshifter in the area and she has been causing much destruction and despair. Orenda attempts to go around the troubled area as he feels tomahawks and arrows are no match against magic. But the Deer Woman is already aware of the warrior's presence in her territory.

If you enjoyed The Bitter Harvest, you'll not want to miss the continuing adventures of Orenda and his small group of heroes.

Spyder Bones

We've heard the tales. The eternal struggle between good and evil. Many religions are based on the concepts. God, Satan, angels and demons; ideals interwoven into our very existence.

Most people have chosen a side, whether they admit it to themselves or not. Many have at least a basic understanding of what is happening. Some have even discovered secrets beyond the veil of what we see. However, there are a few, who not only understand the war, but are in the very thick of it.

This is the story of Spyder Bones, a mystic warrior.

It's the summer of 1969 and Aaron Prescott is a seasoned soldier. After serving one tour of duty in Vietnam as a cavalryman, Aaron returns for a second tour as a combat medic.

Aaron's life revolves around the love of his Vietnamese girlfriend, the danger of combat, and his passion for music. It's not an overly complicated existence, but that's about to change.

Aaron, or Spyder as he is known to his friends, suffers a near death experience during combat. He is subsequently trapped in a comatose state for months. During this time, he is exposed to an unseen war. A spiritual struggle that most people only have a vague awareness of.

Aaron must make some difficult decisions, but, regardless of anything else, he knows his life will never be the same.

Made in the USA
Coppell, TX
13 September 2023

21568124R00085